A Long Way Off

Patricia Marlett

Printed in the United States of America

Published by High Tower Publications

First Edition 2015

ISBN 978-0-9854059-3-9

Acknowledgment

I will always, and forevermore, acknowledge and give thanks to God. I honor, praise, and give the glory to my heavenly Father, for it is by His grace that I am blessed. With the gift He has bestowed upon me, I write in His honor to glorify His name.

Also, deep appreciation to my husband, Mark, for the unwavering love and support he gives as I pursue my passion. You are my rock, I love you.

A special thanks to my niece, Kirsten Allen, a talented Artist and Illustrator, for the cover of this book.

Dedication

This book is dedicated to all the sons and daughters who learn of unconditional love.

Chapter 1

Farming is a way of life in Iowa where the land is premium and farmers are plentiful. Drive the lonely country roads that connect the farms to their small towns, and you will see an outstretch of cornfields as far as the eye can see in either direction. Whether the farm is large or moderate, everyone works diligently to produce a good crop, year after year. For many, it is the only way of life as the tradition is passed down through generations. However to most passing through, there is little fascination with the tall stalks compactly growing with their tassels reaching upwards, ready for harvest. To the farmers, it is an exciting time as they prepare to gather what Mother Nature respectively produced. Some choose to grow a variety of vegetables, but corn remains the main staple.

The farmers within the state share the responsibility of providing all five varieties from the dent and flint which is a hard, colorful corn used primarily for animal feed to the softer kernel which is the sweet, flour, and popcorn type. As in the past, the Abraham Organic Farm grew both the flour and sweet corns, but mostly sweet. Flour corn is converted to baking flour while sweet corn is enjoyed as a vegetable.

The farm is over one-hundred thousand acres with one-third also devoted to cruciferous vegetables. It is proudly known as an organic farm without chemicals sprayed or dusted on the crops, nor pesticides and herbicides used in the soil. They long ago discovered the natural methods of keeping the critters out of their fields. There are two large buildings for processing the corn whereby removing the husk, and stripping the corn from the cob. The byproduct is ground into mulch and reused as a natural fertilizer.

Years ago when William Abraham was a small boy, their large house with its wraparound porch was renovated making the front section of their home into an office with an entrance into a small room that had a receptionist desk, separating two offices on opposing walls. The back section of the house remained the family's living quarters. It was an economic decision rather than building another location on the property for an office.

In its fourth generation, it is considered one of the areas largest and carries the tradition of harvesting the sweetest corn in the Midwest. Annually, sweet corn festivals are held on the property with people traveling from great distances just to sample the many recipes derived from corn with one being the famous sweet corn pie.

William grew up learning to farm and loving the relationship he witnessed between his father and grandfather as they worked the land with pride. Through tough times of drought, or problematic pestilence, the joy never faded, for it simply was in the Abraham blood. He was born with an innate love and respect for farming. Though they accept the Abraham Organic Farm to be one of the farming conglomerates, it wasn't always so. It took years of dedication to develop into the empire it is today producing massive quantities for the largest marketplace, the country. Seasonally, truckloads of produce leave the compound to be shipped to vendors including the grocery stores in their hometown of Calmar.

As a young boy, William worked alongside his father and grandfather willingly sharing in the responsibilities of farming. There wasn't anything he didn't know about crop production. Sometimes he admitted preferring to hang out with his friends after school, but participated in the work without complaint. William was the only son and proudly carried the surname, junior. He grew up with three sisters; therefore, more was expected from him and he took his participation seriously. William stood out in the family in another way as well with sisters favoring their mother's shade of blonde hair and blue eyes, he was the child born of his father's lineage with brown hair and hazel eyes.

His sisters didn't put in the long days of school and work, spending their time visiting friends and involved in extra-circular activities. That was fine with William because he knew that one day the farm would belong to him. Even in their early years, the girls wanted nothing to do with the family business, for they had other plans concerning their future.

When William was ten years old, sitting in grade school behind Marybeth Simpson with her long brunette-braided hair and blue eyes, he knew this was the girl he would marry someday. Of course, Marybeth was unaware of William's intentions. He remained focused on her as they spent the next two years together in a classroom. It wasn't until he was twelve that William mustered the nerve to approach her in the school cafeteria by putting his food tray on the table and sitting next to her. He tilted his head giving her a quick glance, and she smiled at him and cafeteria lunches were never the same.

At her fragile adolescent age, Marybeth was delighted to have a boy interested in her, and yet, a bit timid for the advances. She only understood the relations of sisters being caught in the middle of a younger and older sibling, so boys were off her radar. They seemed too uninhibited for her quiet nature; however, she would be remiss to not finding the attention from William appealing. From that day forward, they shared every lunch exclusively. Though they didn't live in the same part of town, he would walk her to the school bus everyday before barely missing his own. By the time they were sixteen, Marybeth was allowed to go on her first date with William. From his estimation, he had waited six years for this moment when he could accompany Marybeth on a date. It was the highlight of his youth.

In small rural communities, there weren't an exceptional number of things to do, so William took Marybeth to the local hamburger joint for the typical teenager's staple of hamburger, fries, and a milkshake. They sat and talked for hours until time to return her home before sunset. Life was much the same routine from day to day, school and working on the farm with the weekends devoted to his sweetheart.

William knew as he matured into a young man that college wouldn't be necessary. He gave no thought, nor gained any interest in leaving the farm to pursue a degree in agriculture or business management, the two subjects best suited to run an empire. From his viewpoint, like the previous Abraham men, he already had his education from the best tutors, and no schoolbook could teach him more than the experts, his father and grandfather. They never left the farm to acquire an education; therefore, he saw no need to break that chain.

Being a farmer is in the blood, and you're born to the land. You protect, nurture, and respect it like a partnership, and if you treat it well, it will supply for your needs and that is exactly what the Abraham men have always done. To them, it was more than growing vegetables, more than their livelihood, it was a relationship with nature.

In William's senior year of school, his grandfather died suddenly while working in the fields among the employees. It was a hot summer day, and without monitoring his intake of fluids, he quickly became dehydrated. When he passed out, it took too long to get medical help out to the farm, and he simply never regained consciousness. Though an autopsy wasn't performed, the doctor said it was heatstroke that most likely caused a heart attack. He was eighty-nine years old, so the physician's diagnosis seemed plausible.

That left William and his father to take care of the farm. With his grandfather's death, William had a rude awakening that his own father wouldn't always be there. Though his father was only in his early fifties, there would come a day when he would bare the full responsibility of the business. It was a heavy consideration, but one he was prepared to undertake. He had been groomed his entire life for this sole purpose.

Chapter 2

At twenty, William proposed to Marybeth and purposefully waited until the holidays to surprise her with an engagement ring that he strung on a red ribbon tied to the neck of a small brown teddy bear. She cuddled it feeling something rough rub against her cheek, and looking closer saw the ring, and threw herself into his arms. They were married in the spring. In the small town where the population is slightly over one thousand, long engagements weren't necessary, nor did planning a wedding require undo necessities. It was an intimate gathering, more than they could have hoped for. From William's perspective, he had waited ten years for this moment.

William's grandmother died years prior, so when his grandfather passed away, the home his grandfather lived in all his life was given to his grandson. A wood-framed country house completely furnished nestled on the back part of the property. William moved into the house, and lived there a year before bringing his bride to her new home. In his spare time, he worked at upgrading the house with new amenities, things he believed would be pleasing to Marybeth.

He labored diligently beside his father everyday along with the seasonal field employees as the crops were harvested, and the land prepared for new seedlings. Large machines were driven across the acreage to gather the cobs of corn. It was long hard days, but nothing he wasn't accustomed to, and now he had his sweetheart to go home to at the end of the day. This was the life William always dreamt of, working the farmland he cherished and creating memories with Marybeth.

Within the first year of their marriage, Marybeth surprised him with the news of the expansion of their family. When Seth was born, it was another highlight of William's life next to his marriage. No man could have been more proud than he was to become a father. More so, the next generation of the Abraham's was born. As his father, and his father before him, William proudly took his young son with him often as he rode a tractor across the land and pointed out the many facets of the farm. Seth loved being with his dad though too young to understand what his father was telling him.

As Seth grew, William watched through the fascination of his son's eyes an interest that he appreciated. Often Marybeth would chastise William for taking Seth with him to work, but he saw no harm recalling those days when sitting upon his father's lap. All Seth wanted to do was spend his days with his papa in the fields, and at eight, had a one track mind to drive the tractor even when his short legs and small feet couldn't reach the pedals. William saw himself in his son, and understood what it must have been like for his own father.

William and Marybeth wanted several children, but it didn't seem to be in their future to have more. It was a disappointment Marybeth struggled with daily, a heartache she tried to disguise. William was more accepting of the matter because he had a son to carry on the family name which was of the upmost importance. He tried to console his wife when times arose and it weighed heaviest on her heart, but as the years passed, she was inclined to not dwell on what couldn't be, even though she secretly thought of it often.

Life was good to them as William, alongside his father and with his son, Seth, prepared the land for the next harvest. Eight years into their marriage, and much to her astonishment, Marybeth had a second surprise for her husband. She couldn't have been more elated to share the news that they were having another baby, believing all those years of praying was finally coming to fruition. William was amazed and grateful to see Marybeth beaming with happiness again.

In the same year that Jacob was born, William's father died of a massive heart attack. Just like his father, William senior was in the heart of his farm when it was his time to leave this earth. At twenty-eight, William became the sole proprietor of the Abraham Organic Farm, and it was up to him to carry on the empire. He and Marybeth with their two sons moved into his parent's house. She took care of the home, the baby, and the bookkeeping for the business while he and Seth worked outside, content with the life they were making together.

Marybeth coddled her newborn, for Jacob was a sweet and endearing infant, favoring her brunette hair and blue eyes. She finally felt their life was complete with two children. With Seth spending most of the time with his father, the opportunity to have him around the house as he grew was limited, but Marybeth thought it cruel to withhold something her son loved so much, and didn't prohibit him from being outside. Seth, at nine, spent time in school, or outdoors alongside his father while Marybeth and Jacob remained in the house. The family routine was quickly established, and the years passed in contentment as William and Marybeth believed their life was perfect.

On a cold wintery day with snow-blanketed fields and icy roads, Marybeth drove into town as she often did. Having lived her entire life in Calmar, she knew how to navigate along the countryside; however, a truck passing through the area did not, and plowed into her car as she drove through a four-way intersection with a yellow blinking light. The driver never slowed and with no time to react, she was gone in an instant.

The Abraham men were never the same after that fatal day. William fell into a deep depression losing the love of his life. His world revolved around Marybeth, and now she was gone to him forever, and didn't think he could go on without her, even though he had his sons. He gave no thought to the daily requirements of running the farm, for it didn't matter without his sweetheart, so William spent his days roaming the house with no interest in living.

Marybeth was only forty-nine, leaving Seth age twenty-eight and Jacob at nineteen to take over the daily responsibilities of managing the business while their father grieved. As the older son, Seth took on the duties of managing the farm while Jack handled the accounting just as his mother had done. The evening hours were a difficult time for them when the personal turmoil was most apparent, and the mourning each was experiencing over Marybeth's death was pronounced. William often gave an appearance at the dinner table still in pajamas and unshaven, and his sons privately wondered when was the last time he had bathed.

As they settled into a routine, Jake decided to leave home for college in a nearby city to major in finance with a minor in business management, believing the knowledge he would acquire in school could be beneficial. Jacob realized this left Seth alone to care for the farm, but Seth wasn't going to prevent Jake from doing what he wanted to do. Jake committed to returning home often and especially for the holidays.

Seth hired a business manager, Margaret Grey, to handle the accounting. Jake agreed it was necessary for someone to take his place, and before he left, he spent time teaching her the job. Seth realized he wasn't superman, he couldn't work the fields by day and manage the books at night. He wanted to hire someone older and stable, and she came to the interview with a solid resume. Margaret became an intricate member of the family's business, and an unshakable influence. She often asked to be called Maggie, but everyone always referred to her as Mrs. Grey and it stuck.

In her mid-fifties, short and slightly plump with red hair and green eyes, she carried more of a matronly appearance than that of a manager, but her previous work performance was impeccable. She was energetic and friendly, something that was a bonus dealing with customers. Immediately, Margaret witnessed the pain in the Abraham's, and her heart was heavy for these men and their loss. She intended to rectify matters as best she could without overstepping liberties.

He also hired a housekeeper to tend to the basic chores of keeping the house clean, doing the grocery shopping, preparing meals and placing them in the freezer, making it convenient for the men to have something healthy to eat. It was another responsibility Seth needed to delegate and good judgment on his part to hire Dorothy Owens who was a perfectionist. Dorothy was a tall slender woman with short black hair and dark brown eyes in her late forties who beamed with energy.

Seth was forever grateful for the longstanding commitment of Samuel Parkinson, the foreman his father hired years prior. When it came to supervising the men and getting the work done on schedule, Sam never failed. He came to the farm straight out of college with an agricultural degree and was hired on the spot. Sam was a tall slender black man in his late thirties who had become an important member of the Abraham farm.

Everything fell upon Seth's shoulders, but he could handle it and made the necessary decisions and changes to keep the farm afloat believing it was temporary. He expected his father to overcome his depression and things would get back to normal, but in the meantime, he had help.

It took William over a year to pull himself out of his despair with constant coercion from his oldest son and Mrs. Grey. She prepared his lunch, forced him into conversation, and slowly William began to show interest in the farm again. He sat behind his desk and stared at the wall uncertain what to do, for so much time had lapsed, and he didn't know the state of affairs of his business, but realized he needed to start getting involved again. Marybeth would want him to move forward with his life.

Mrs. Grey secretly smiled to herself, knowing he was finally coming out of the black abyss. Late one afternoon, Seth walked into the office to pick up some papers and noticed the light shining through the glass door of his father's office. He turned to see Mrs. Grey smiling. Seth smiled in return, and changed his direction towards the office door and went in without knocking.

"Dad, are you all right," Seth inquired, puzzled.

William looked at his son.

"I will be."

Seth took a seat at one of the two chairs in front of the oversize mahogany desk.

"You've been gone for a while. It will be good to have you back, I've missed you."

"I've been sitting here thinking, and I realize these past several months, I've put an enormous burden on you and Jake. I feel bad about that."

Their father was including Jake in the maintenance of the farm, and Seth didn't see that as being fair.

"Dad, you do realize Jake went to college."

"Yes, I understand he wanted to better himself."

"I've been handling the business while he's been gone."

"I know that, Seth, and you've done a great job keeping things going in my absence, but you don't need my recognition for your hard work, you'll always have it."

"I appreciate you saying that."

Seth wanted his father to understand his dedication.

"When I look at you, I see a younger version of myself. How can I not be proud of your loyalty to the family business, and to me?"

"I've always been beside you, Dad, and always will be."

"I understand that, and wouldn't want to run this farm without you by my side."

"That's all I wanted to hear, welcome back."

Seth left the office and went out to the barn pleased to see his father had finally overcome his depression. Maybe now things would get back to normal.

In the following days, William began the journey of recovery by throwing himself into the business. Mrs. Grey was delighted to show him the purchase orders, financial statements, and enlighten him on the daily functions of what he had missed. She explained how well the farm was doing financially, and expounded on Seth's ability to manage the business during his absence.

Jacob came home unexpectedly on a Friday afternoon to find his father standing beside Mrs. Grey. William looked up when he heard the door open to see his youngest son walk in, and immediately rushed towards Jake pulling him into a tight embrace.

"Jake, my boy, it's so good to see you," William said with emotion.

"Good to see you too, Dad. I didn't expect you to be in the office."

With his father taking an active role in the business again, Jake made it a point to return home often to visit, but made no attempt to get involved in the farm, not being current on matters.

After Jacob graduated, he was excited to apply his expertise and wizardry in finance to the business. He believed his best contribution to the farm was implementing strategic methodologies of streamlining production in both efficiency and cost-effectiveness, work smarter not harder was his motto. He took the small unimposing office across from his father's, and worked alongside Mrs. Grey. He had plans for running a more proficient business, and a quicker way of earning money.

William was pleased to see Jake participating in the business. Seth enjoyed working outdoors while Jake preferred to be in an office. Jake spent most of his time on the computer devising methods of making money. He had learned in college about stocks, bonds, and mutual funds and became fascinated with the subject. He was constantly studying various websites, trying to perfect the skill of buying, selling, and trading. Almost to an obsession, he followed trends and made small investments, something he began in college. He was determined to show his father an easier way to earn money, and not work so hard in crop production.

It wasn't long before Jake became antsy for something more exciting and challenging as life on the farm was too mundane and redundant. He enjoyed talking about the stock market and making money, but could never draw his father or brother into conversations on the subject. He was eager to discuss the things he had learned in college, but neither showed an interest. Often at dinner, Jake shared information about a company he was studying, but the subject would quickly revert to discussing matters concerning the farm.

Unlike Seth, the farm wasn't Jake's passion as much as he tried to make it so for his father's sake. He began to spend more time away and less doing his job, and it was noticed by everyone. Someone had to take up the slack for him not being there, and it fell on Seth and Mrs. Grey, but they were accustomed to doing it while he was in college. It was expected that Jake would settle into his responsibilities, but he didn't. He came and went as he pleased, and felt he owed no one an explanation.

Jake continued to talk with his father about his ideas, but felt he wasn't being taken seriously. In time, Jake became more distant from the family believing them to be fools for working so hard when he could show them a better way. If they weren't going to accept his suggestions of making money through investments, then he would show them how to simplify and streamline production methods for the business, another subject he learned in college.

One of his many recommendations was upgrading the business accounting system with new software. Practically every evening at the dinner table, Jake offered ideas hoping his recommendations would be accepted, but they were ignored.

"I know what I'm talking about," Jake said.

"Yeah, with your fancy education. This farm has grown to what it is today through hard work. Don't need a college education to know how to operate it," Seth declared, tired of Jake's big ideas but lack of commitment.

"You're just jealous of what I have accomplished."

"You've got that wrong, I didn't stop you from going to college."

"Then why isn't anyone listening to me, and using the knowledge I've learned?"

"This farm has survived generations without outside help," Seth told him.

"Since I have the education, why not use it?" Jake said, pressing his point.

"Don't need it," Seth said.

Every evening it was the same discussion, and Jake had grown weary of trying to convince them, and accepted that it was no use. William saw the unease in his youngest son, and only hoped that Jake would settle into his heritage and work alongside Seth, but had his concerns as Jake was absent more often then not.

Chapter 3

Jake lost all interest in the family business believing there was a better way to earn money, and a more exciting life in the process. He wanted to do more, find some excitement and purpose other than counting bins of corn. He left the farm in the afternoon, and often didn't return until the next morning which became his daily routine, and no one questioned his whereabouts. William could only imagine the lifestyle his youngest was carving out for himself, while Seth grew angry at the dismissive attitude of his younger brother.

On one such occasion, Jake was driving down the dirt road on their property that led to the house. It is a long and winding lane defined with white picket fencing on either side and an overgrowth of trees and shrubs. So accustomed to the scenery, he gave no attention to the surroundings. From a distance, Jake could see his father, Seth, and Samuel standing next to the barn, talking. Whatever they were discussing, it didn't look good, and he wasn't going to get drawn into the middle of it, so he maneuvered the company SUV off the lane and pulled up to the opposite side of the house.

He was soon to learn what the commotion was all about. Vendor trucks hadn't arrived to pick up the produce, and they were debating what to do about the problem. Unbeknownst to anyone, Jake made a managerial decision and upgraded the accounting software before confirming with his father. He figured if no one was going to listen to him, he'd show them, and then they'd understand what he was trying to tell them. However, after making such a change, havoc broke out as production came to a screeching halt. Men were standing around waiting for trucks to show up to haul off the produce, but the purchase requisitions were unaccessible and vendors couldn't be notified. It set Seth in a rage that William could not fault him for.

"The men aren't doing much," Sam told them.

"We had a glitch," Seth replied.

"They're just standing around, it's frustrating. What do you want me to tell them?"

"Take them some water, and tell them to relax while we get this sorted out."

"Alright."

Samuel walked away trying not to show his own frustration.

"You have got to do something about Jake," Seth told his father.

"What do you propose I do?"

"I don't know, but he's got to be productive, and show up on time. This mistake is going to cost us."

"I'll talk to him."

"Has anybody seen Jake," Seth yelled, looking around as he left his father's side.

William watched him for a moment before going into the office. He hoped Jake would be there because he needed an explanation, this was his responsibility. Men were ready to put in a full days labor.

Deliberately bypassing this scene, Jake walked into the office door with his sunglasses covering his eyes. Mrs. Grey looked up from her work and warned him.

"I would hide if I were you. Your brother has been looking for you, and he's in one of his moods."

"Well, that's a shock, I'll be in my office."

Jake sat down at the small desk situated in a corner with his back to the entrance. Uninterested, he thumbed through a stack of papers before tossing them into a basket. The investment book he had been reading was on the desk, and he reached for it as William stood in the doorway.

"Jake, you changed the invoicing program," his father said without preamble.

"I told you I was going to," Jake replied, not turning to address his father as he flipped through the pages.

"You did it even though I asked you not to."

"I know, and now we have a more efficient system."

"That's not acceptable."

"Okay, what do you want to do, Dad. You want to fire me?"

He turned to face his father.

"We're not selling widgets, Jake. We're selling the best grains and produce in the state, and this program that you brought in..."

Jake cut him off.

"The new program is faster than the previous one, so what's the problem. I've been telling you about it for weeks."

"The problem is no one knows how to use it, so we missed a large shipment this morning because you haven't properly trained..."

Again, Jake interrupted.

"Do you expect me to do everything around here?"

"No, but I expect you to do your job."

"That's exactly what I am doing."

"Part of your responsibility is to inform the rest of us, and if training is required, do it first."

William shook his head and sighed. Jake watched his father walk away, disappointed. He contemplated his father's words when his thoughts were interrupted by Seth.

"Well, you're up early," Seth said sarcastically, standing in the same place his father vacated minutes earlier.

"You've got to be kidding," Jake said under his breath.

"Mrs. Grey, why did you let him in?" he yelled out to her.

"What's the matter? Someone not doing their job."

"If you are here to chastise me, Dad beat you to it."

"You know, we couldn't access the purchase orders."

"I know that."

"Means, we've got guys standing around doing nothing because vendors won't be here."

"I heard that too."

"It cost us money, Jake," Seth said, raising his voice.

"I know."

"This could have been avoided if you'd gotten here on time today instead of rolling in late, hungover. It could have been corrected, but now it's too late to do anything about it."

"You want me to agree, fine. You're right, anything else?"

"You're pathetic," Seth said under his breath before walking away, disgusted.

Jake turned around in his chair, and focused on the computer monitor. He blew out a deep breath of air, and again, was interrupted by Mrs. Grey.

"I told you to hide."

"Why don't you ever knock?"

"Why should I?"

"So you don't give me a heart attack, Mrs. Grey. I tend to daydream and believe it or not, you're not the girl I'm on the beach with."

I like beaches," she said, playing along.

"Not going to happen."

"Well, we've got another problem. The engine parts for the tractor have not arrived, and the acreage in the south field is scheduled for planting tomorrow."

"Okay, tell Seth to have Samuel take care of it, delegate some responsibility."

"Need I remind you that this is something else that could have been avoided."

"If I had shown up to work on time, I get it."

"The rest of us have been here since seven. Jake, you come in late and leave early, and no one is objecting to you having a life outside the farm, but we have to work as a team, and one member can't make changes and not make the others aware," she told him, motherly.

"So you do have something to say, forget it. Call Benwood and get the parts from them."

"Benwood, no."

"If we go with Benwood, we can get the engine fixed today."

"They use cheap materials that won't last one season."

"You said yourself, we need it running."

"Seth won't like it."

"I don't care what Seth thinks, just do it."

"Well, someone is testy," she replied, walking away.

Mrs. Grey placed the call confirming a mechanic from Benwood would be out, and parts installed within the next few hours.

Jake realized he erred in changing the system without informing anyone, and sequestered himself in his office the remainder of the morning, grateful to be left alone. Those who had something to say had already done so, leaving him feeling deflated. At lunchtime, Jake went into the kitchen to find his father sitting at the table eating a sandwich, and opened the refrigerator to grab the one in a paper bag, and sat down at the table.

"Have you given any thought to our conversation this morning?" William asked.

"The one where everything is my fault."

"It was irresponsible to change the program that no one can access the accounts."

"I told you I was going to install a new software program," Jake said, defensively.

"Yes, and if you recall, I suggested we hold off and try it later in the off-season when business is slower. It would give everyone an opportunity to learn the new system."

"You put me in this position to make decisions that would financially benefit the business, and that's what I'm doing, but no one is listening."

"You did it even though I asked you to wait. I wasn't declining the idea, but suggesting it be done at another time."

"I'm your son. I thought you trusted me to make decisions that were in the best interest of the farm."

"Of course, I trust you. This is not about trust, but team effort. We have to work together. Making sole decisions that are not unanimously agreed with a plan of implementation is not beneficial for business. It is not acceptable, you are not a team of one. This new program may not be what the company needs right now."

"I'm trying to make this place more efficient. This new program is ten times faster."

"No one knows how to use it because you haven't trained anyone on the software."

"Do I really have to do everything around here?" Jake argued, defensively.

"No, but if you are going to make changes without my consent, then at least tell everyone and train them."

"What do you want me to do, Dad? You want me to leave?"

William watched his son, not surprised by the direction of Jake's thoughts.

"No, Jake. Why would you even think that?"

William caught the fact that twice in a matter of hours, his son had mentioned leaving. Something was on Jake's mind.

Jake shrugged his shoulders, and took a bite of the sandwich.

"Are you feeling okay? You look pale," William asked.

"I'm fine."

"I'll have Mrs. Grey get you some aspirin."

"I said, I'm fine."

"We'll talk more later. I should let everyone go home, there's no reason to keep them hanging around any longer."

Seth came in and opened the refrigerator door to find his sandwich missing, and walked over to grab it from Jake.

"This is mine, make your own."

Seth stood at the counter, and took a bite of the sandwich.

"We've paid men to stand around all morning, thanks to you," Seth told him.

"I've already gotten that memo, and besides, I don't answer to you," Jake replied.

"We have a day without production because of you."

"How many times today must I hear it?"

"Your decision to change things has cost money. I guess that doesn't concern you," Seth said, driving his point.

"You've already said that, besides it can be fixed. It's not a big deal."
Jake defended his position.

"Losing money is a big deal, and it could've been avoided if you hadn't changed to a program that no one can use."

"Alright, I get it. Lay off."

"I'm glad you're having fun now, because it's all going to end soon."

"What? A threat from big brother."

"I don't make threats."

"I've had enough of this," Jake said, under his breath.

Jake got up from the table having lost his appetite, and left the kitchen feeling no one appreciated him.

Chapter 4

That was the final straw for Jake. It was time to move on, so the next day, again at lunchtime, he spoke with his father. It seemed to be the best time to find him alone, uninterrupted. He deliberately took Seth's sandwich from the refrigerator, the one he always made the night before, and sat down at the table. As he unwrapped it, Jake expressed his thoughts.

"No one appreciates what I do around here."

"That's not true. It's important when you make changes to let us all know. We can't afford to have too many days like yesterday. You need to communicate better," William told him.

"Would it make a difference? I've been trying to tell you for months how to make money without working so hard, but you won't listen. There is an easier way."

"I appreciate that, but I don't see the stock market as the way."

"I can show you, it's simple."

Jake was always excited to talk about his favorite subject. He studied the market trends daily, and faithfully believed he could make money in abundance. When he saw the look in his father's eyes, he knew he wasn't interested. Dejected, Jake withdrew making any further comments and got to the point.

"I think it's time for me to move out."

"You're gone most of the time, so why do you feel a need to leave?"

"It's nothing to do with you, Dad, but this isn't my life."

"What is your life?"

"I don't know yet, but hopefully something more interesting than vegetables."

"I admit farming isn't glamorous, but it's noble work we do and necessary. Someone has to produce the crops for the country."

"I know that, and I know it's your dream to have me stay and work on the farm, but it's not mine. I don't want the same things you do. I want to choose how I live my life. For once, I would like to go out and have a good time, and not come home to a sermon."

This conversation had been coming for some time as William witnessed the discontent in his youngest son.

"Jake, I'm not expecting you to be perfect, but we have to work together as a family."

"There is a world out there, and I want to explore it and experience the adventure because surely there is none around here. I need to move on with my life."

Though William understood his son's restlessness, hearing his words aloud hurt. William had known nothing but the farm his entire life, and found it hard to accept that Jake had no interest in carrying on the family business. Jacob was a dreamer, but he also couldn't deny that he was a young man with his own ambitions, desiring to make a life other than the one he proposed for him.

"Are you seriously thinking of leaving?"

"It's not a rash decision."

William lowered his head and pondered the situation for a moment. Seth walked into the kitchen, and opened the refrigerator door to find his sandwich missing, again, and glanced to see Jake eating it.

"Glad you found time to take a break today. That's my lunch you're eating."

"Make yourself another one."

This time Seth didn't grab the half eaten sandwich, and took condiments to make a fresh one.

"You're coming with me today to talk to the customers."

"Why?"

"Because they are going to be mad, and I'm tired of covering for you. There is no produce for their stores, and the reason for that is you. It was your mistake, so you should be the one to talk to them."

"I don't deal with customers, too bad."

"What exactly do you do here? Half the day is gone before you show up, and you leave before everyone else, and to think you get paid."

"I wouldn't expect you to understand what I do, especially since you never went to college," Jake said, wanting to jab at his brother with the best arsenal he had.

"No, I had to stay here and work. I didn't have the luxury of wasting time hanging out at parties and skipping classes," Seth said, tired of Jake's laziness.

"You are the only one who feels that way. Could it be because you want the freedom to do the things I do."

"You wish," Seth said, staring at his brother with contempt.

Jake stood up in front of Seth.

"Thank you so much for sticking around because we all know how hard it is to find someone who can drive a tractor."

Jake knew that would further infuriate him. Seth pushed Jake in the upper shoulder and pointed a finger at him.

"You're a disgrace to this family," Seth told him, angrily.

"Seth, enough," William said, sternly.

"Admit it, your jealous. You always have been," Jake yelled.

"Come on, show me how jealous I am."

"You are jealous."

"To think I agreed to you going to college. What a waste."

"That's because you want it."

"Stop!" William hollered to be heard above their voices.

Seth ignored his father's warning.

"Why don't you just leave? Go! What are you waiting for? Make all of our lives easier, just get out."

"Maybe I'll do that, but it won't be for your sake."

Jake glanced at his father with an 'I'm-out-of-here' expression. William sighed as he watched Jake leave the room, realizing there would be no talking him out of leaving after the blowup with Seth, and it broke his heart. He finished lunch in silence.

Later that day, William walked into Jake's office finding him working on the computer.

"Are you okay?"

"I'm fine," Jake replied, punching the keys on the keypad.

William sat down next to the desk.

"I've switched back to the old invoicing program."

"I appreciate that."

William paused.

"You know Seth, he's got that hot temper."

"I know, but he's got a point. I don't know why I'm still here. I want to leave," Jake told his father.

"You can't just do that."

"I can. I don't think my life will ever be here, I want more. I quit, Dad."

William studied his son understanding his decision was final.

"How will you afford to live on your own?"

"Maybe we should talk about a severance package. I've worked on the farm and went to school to get an education for the business, so surely that must account for some financial consideration."

"It usually doesn't work that way."

"I need some money to get started, and make some investments."

"How much are you asking for?"

Jake paused, looking at his father.

"What about my inheritance? The money you stashed away in a portfolio. I take that now, I can double it, or more by the time I would have received it."

"I see you've given this some thought. What I have set aside for you and Seth along with this farm is all I have for you when I'm gone."

"I understand, but I can make more."

It was a substantial amount to hand over to a son he wasn't sure could handle himself.

"I'll think about it."

"Okay, let me know because either way, I'm gone when I get my stuff together."

"I suppose I can't talk you into staying, even for a while longer."

"No Dad, it wouldn't change anything, nothing ever changes around here."

"You've made up your mind."

"I've thought about this for some time since college. I tried, but it just isn't working for me."

Jake got up and left his father sitting there. William slowly walked out of Jake's office.

"Mrs. Grey, would you get Mr. Farris on the phone."

"Sure, will do."

William went to his office and closed the door. He had much to consider since there would be no persuading Jake to stay. The question now was how much money to give him.

Chapter 5

He spoke to his longtime friend and financial advisor, Clifford Farris, and arranged for him to stop by the house the next morning having explained the urgency of the matter. Cliff is a short man in his early sixties with a receding brown hairline. He wore wired-rimmed glasses and a gray suit. As they sat at the dining room table waiting for Jake, they made light conversation.

"How's your rose garden?" Cliff asked.

"The garden is beautiful. That was Marybeth's, and I try to take care of it," William said, thinking of his wife.

"I haven't been out this way in some time. The farm is looking prosperous."

"Can't complain."

"Boys doing okay?"

"Seth and Jake are fine."

Jake walked into the room to find his father and Mr. Farris sitting at the table, and reached out to shake his hand before sitting opposite him.

"Jake, I haven't seen you in a long time."

"It's been awhile, so how does this work?' Jake asked, glancing at his father. They had not spoken further about the matter of money.

"There's a few steps we have to take," Mr. Farris said.

"How many steps can there be?"

William spoke up.

"I've decided to give you the entire amount, but understand this is all your inheritance except for your share of the farm."

"How much are we talking?" Jake asked.

William looked at Cliff and nodded. He opened a manilla folder and took the document, placed it on the table, and slid it towards Jake. Without touching the paper, Jake leaned forward for a closer look.

"That figure at the bottom of the page is your inheritance, and you'll get it in one check, but there is some paperwork involved to complete this transaction," Mr. Farris explained.

Jake focused on the amount.

"Are you sure you want to do this?" William asked.

"Yes, I told you I was."

"I'm your father, I love you, and just want to make sure you'll be alright."

"I'm an adult and can take of myself."

William sighed.

"Cliff, go ahead and draw up the papers."

"I'll have them ready first thing in the morning."

Mr. Farris retrieved the document, placed it in the folder, and put it inside the briefcase that was on the floor and stood up to leave.

"I'll walk you out, Cliff," William said.

Jake remained seated at the table smiling to himself. His new life was about to begin, and he could hardly contain himself. He was shocked to see how much money he was leaving with. He was a rich man.

Mr. Farris was at the house early. After gathering around the same table, Cliff took out the necessary papers for Jake to sign before handing him a check. Jake leaned back in his chair threading his fingers in his hands behind his head with a big grin on his face, then took the check and stared at it, mesmerized.

"Is this for real?" Jake asked, still astonished.

"Yes, it is and you have your father's intuitiveness to thank for setting up two IRA's for you and Seth years ago," Mr. Farris explained.

"Understand Jake, this is all of your cash inheritance. The portfolio that your father established for you will be closed once you endorse this check. It will not continue to accrue funds in the future, this is it in its entirety," he continued.

Jake didn't even glance at his father, but remained focused on the check.

"I understand."

William watched his son closely, saddened that Jake felt an urgency to leave. He shouldn't take it personally, but he did. It bothered him that Jake defied the traditions of farming and him. He would never prevent his boys from pursuing their dreams; however, he would miss his son and could only pray for Jake's wellbeing, and that someday he would return home.

Jake signed the papers and the check was officially released to him. Reaching across the table to shake Mr. Farris' hand, he turned to see Seth had witnessed the transaction.

"I'm out of here, you get your wish."

"Not soon enough."

"A fool and his money," Seth said, looking at his father.

Jake never thanked his father for the inheritance, nor did he look at him before leaving the room. William took his son's behavior in stride, but deep inside he was disappointed.

Jake stayed in his bedroom the remainder of the day sorting through the things he wanted to take. Looking around the room, he realized there was nothing of this life he cherished. He placed clothes and toiletries into a small suitcase along with his laptop, a few books, and compact disk of his favorite music into a duffel bag. Jake planned to stop by the bank and cash the check on his way out in the morning. Thanks to Mr. Farris' forethought, William's bank was notified of the necessity for a large sum of money to process the transaction.

His final appearance at dinner felt like the last supper, the atmosphere was stagnant. Later that evening, he took a walk on the property stopping periodically to watch the cornstalks gently swaying in the evening breeze. Unexpectedly, his father walked up beside him.

"Beautiful sight, isn't it?" William said, looking out over his land with pride.

"To you, but not to me," Jake replied, honestly.

"This is all I have ever known, seems I was destined to follow in my father's footsteps."

"I know, Dad. I do respect you for that, but now I need you to accept what I must do."

William remained silent for a few seconds before responding.

"I have a great deal of respect for you, Jake. You are my son, and I will always love you. Wherever you go and whatever you do to find yourself, I want you to know that I'll be here for you."

Jake looked at his father's profile seeing a glistening in his eyes; however, his desire to leave was greater than his father's feelings to stay.

"You don't have to worry about me, I'll be fine."

William looked deeply into his son's eyes.

"I will worry about you."

William walked away leaving his son alone.

Jake was given a somber farewell the next morning. Mrs. Grey gave him a teary-eyed hug wishing him well. He embraced his father and noticed Seth on the porch, watching.

"Do you know where you're going to live?"

"No, not yet, but I'll figure it out."

William reached in his pants pocket and pulled out an old pocket watch, handing it to Jake.

"Here, take this."

Jake looked at the watch.

"This was grandpa's watch. It's the only thing you have left of your father, I can't take it."

"I want you to have it. Maybe it'll let you know when it's time to come home."

"Does it even work?"

"It works, take it."

He accepted the watch and flipped it open to see that it was set to the right time.

"Thanks."

"A lot of people will miss you, Jake."

"No one is going to miss me, Dad. It's better for everyone that I leave."

"You're not doing this for us, and I will miss you, son."

"You're right."

Jake didn't want this to be a prolonged departure.

"I've got to go."

"Okay, you drive careful."

William didn't ask Jake to contact him when he got settled, and his son didn't offer. He understood that Jake wanted a clean break. Jake glanced at Seth and threw up his hand, but his brother didn't reciprocate. He climbed behind the wheel of his pickup truck, rolled down the window, and gave one final wave before driving off the property. Seth turned and walked inside the house with an attitude of good riddance.

William watched the trail of dust from his son's truck. He wondered what would happen to his youngest. Unable to see the truck bumper, William turned and walked into the house to be confronted by Seth.

"It's not right that Jake takes off with that kind of money. Come on Dad, you just handed him a million bucks, that's crazy," Seth said in disgust.

"It was his money."

"Then give him a portion, if you feel the need to give him something. He'll blow every penny of it, you just wait and see."

"That may be, but it's his to do whatever he wants."

"You made that too easy for him, he should have gone penniless."

"Why?"

"He never lifted a finger around here, and you reward him with a chunk of change."

"I would do the same for you, Seth."

They dropped the conversation remembering Mrs. Grey was present. She was sitting behind her desk dabbing at her eyes with a Kleenex.

"I will miss that boy," she confided.

"We all will," William replied.

"Not me," Seth confessed, walking away.

William and Mrs. Grey watched him leave.

"Surely, he'll miss his brother. Who's he going to pick on now that Jake is gone," she said, unconcerned for her outspokenness.

"You have a point."

There was much catching up to do with the loss of a day of production.

"Now that we are on the old accounting program, let's see if we can get some extra men to help for a couple of days."

"I'll get right on it."

William sat down behind his desk. Papers everywhere, a backlog of work, but his mind wouldn't think of these things as his thoughts strayed to his son. He put his face in his hands and prayed.

Chapter 6

Jake didn't glance in the rearview mirror as he drove away feeling as though he had waited his entire life for this moment. Without a care in the world and a wad of cash, he was chasing after his destiny, and it didn't matter the destination because he intended to make it happen. He planned to double his inheritance, and return home for a visit to show them his success.

When Jake came to a fork in the road, he took a quarter and flipped it in the air. From this point of origin, the option was to travel north or south.

"Heads to the South, tails to the North," he said aloud as he caught it, and slapped the coin on the back of his hand.

"Alright, south it is."

Jake drove until the gas gauge read empty and stopped to fill the tank, grabbed a bite to eat at a diner, and got behind the wheel again intending to put more miles behind him before reaching a permanent place. As the sun was setting, he pulled off the main highway to a roadside hotel for the night. He didn't know the name of the town, and it didn't matter for first thing in the morning he'd be gone.

Driving due south, the road signs indicated he was traveling towards Springfield, Missouri. He continued towards the city noticing the downtown skyline from a distance, and thought it a good place to stop and explore. As he approached, he rolled down the window to inhale the many complex odors that are specific to any city, wanting to experience it all.

Impressed with what he saw, Jake pulled into the circular entrance of the Lincoln Plaza Hotel in downtown, and turned his truck over to the valet. With his suitcase and duffel bag hung over his right shoulder, Jake walked inside the enormous marbled lobby and straight to the matching counter to reserve a suite. After obtaining a room key and taking the elevator to the tenth floor, he entered a massive room with contemporary geometric-designed fabric furniture, and placed his suitcase and bag on a nearby chair. He drew back the sheer drapes exposing a large window overlooking the skyline.

"Amazing."

Jake looked around the room before going to the kitchenette, opening the refrigerator to find four bottled waters. Beside the compact refrigerator was a wet-bar with numerous sampler bottles of various liquors.

"Nice."

He took his luggage into the separate bedroom and threw it onto the king-sized bed with its plush comforter and removed the few items, putting clothes into the closet and toiletries in the bathroom. Upon returning to the main room, he grabbed a fashion magazine on the coffee table, and sat flipping pages, stopping at an advertisement for a watch, a very expensive one. Jake made a quick decision to leave the hotel in search of a jeweler.

Surely there would be a jewelry store among the downtown shops and took his time strolling further into the congested area. Jake stopped at a cafe for a sandwich and iced tea before venturing in and out of the speciality stores. The displays in the windows intrigued him, and he lingered looking through each pane of glass. Most were women's fashions, boutiques, and trinkets shops. Within a half-mile radius of walking, Jake came across a jeweler. It was exactly what he was hoping to find and went inside to study the glass-encased items. An attractive young woman with long auburn hair and chocolate brown eyes approached from behind the counter.

"May I help you find something?" she asked.

"Maybe you can. I'm interested in a watch, a Hublot Tourbillon Solo."

"Follow me around the counter, and I'll be glad to show you our selection. That is a very impressive watch, and you're in luck, for it's one of our top sellers."

Jake walked alongside reaching a glass enclosure that housed four expensive designs. He studied the case spotting the exact one he saw in the magazine and pointed to it.

"I'd like to see that one in the back row," he said, before giving her a chance to unlock the case.

The young sales woman placed a black velvet platform on the glass countertop and removed the watch from its base, spreading the band wide on the smooth canvas. Jake stared at it and with his right index finger, lightly touched the band.

"Let's see how it looks on you. Give me your wrist, so I can fasten it."

Jake slipped his jacket sleeve back on his right arm and extended his wrist, watching her place the band and clasp it.

"Looks nice on you, and it fits perfectly."

Jake is focused on the watch.

"Yes, it does."

He's fascinated by the appeal of such an expensive and tangible item.

"How much is it?"

"One hundred and five thousand dollars, plus tax, of course."

"I'll take it."

"May I help you with anything else today?"

Inquisitive, Jake asked.

"What is your favorite?"

"My favorite is a heart-shaped diamond necklace that I obsess over everyday I'm here."

"Show me."

She walked to another glass case and removed a beautiful diamond-embedded heart hanging from a platinum chain, resting on a purple neck board.

"It's stunning. If I could, I'd get it for myself."

"It is beautiful," Jake said, watching her face as she focused on the necklace.

She traced her left index finger lightly stroking the chain.

"It has a pristine three-quarter karat, brilliant diamond cut inlayed in pure titanium."

"Why is this your favorite?"

"I love the heart."

"How much is it?"

"Twenty-four thousand."

"Really."

"Yes, this is a perfect gift for your wife, or girlfriend," she said, attempting to make another sale.

Earnings were by commission, and so far she was doing good.

"I'll take that too."

"Perfect, shall I wrap it for you?"

"No need," Jake said, pulling out a wad of cash from his pants pocket.

She rang up the two items.

"Would you like to wear the watch, or shall I put it in a box?"

"I'll wear it."

She told him the total, and he counted the money. She recounted the amount and gave him change along with a receipt.

"Give me a minute, and I'll gift wrap the necklace."

He stopped her from reaching for it.

"This is for you," he told her.

"What?"

"The necklace is yours."

"Why would you buy it for me?" she asked, astonished.

"I felt generous today, and besides, I imagine it would look lovely around your neck."

She blushed and smiled at him.

"Is this for real?"

"Absolutely."

"No, seriously. Is this Candid Camera? Are you wearing a hidden microphone?" she asked, peering over his shoulder to see if someone is standing behind him with a camera.

"It's the real deal, I assure you."

She stared at him as Jake took his purchase off of the purple velvet base.

"Turn around," he instructed her.

She turned with her back to him, and Jake slipped the necklace over her head with the small heart resting on her skin, and fastened it. Her hand reached to touch the heart while turning to smile at him.

"I can't believe you did this. You don't even know me," she said, surprised by his generosity.

"Pretty necklace for a beautiful woman."

"Oh my gosh, thank you."

She continued to fondle the necklace.

"This is unbelievable," she told him.

"What are you doing this evening? I'd like to take you out, if you aren't married."

Jake didn't see a ring on her finger.

"I'd love to go out with you," she replied with a big smile.

"Give me your address, and I'll pick you up at seven, but I think I should know your name."

"Beverly."

"Do you have a last name?"

"Watson."

"It's a pleasure to meet you, Beverly Watson. I'm Jake Abraham."

Beverly jotted down her address and phone number on a piece of paper, and handed it to him. Jake shoved it in his pocket.

"I'll see you later," he said, walking out of the store.

"Yes, you will."

Jake stepped onto the sidewalk and paused for a moment to watch the people passing in both directions. He pulled back his sleeve and studied the watch, pleased with his purchase. Next stop was a clothing store he discovered a few blocks on the opposite side of the street and spent the next two hours being fitted for a new wardrobe.

Chapter 7

After taking his purchases back to the hotel, Jake ventured out on another quest to buy a vehicle. He wasn't going to take his date out for the evening in a pickup truck. The valet brought his truck to the front of the hotel. Jake drove towards the outskirts of the city where he passed a dealership on his way into downtown. He turned onto the large lot, parked, and strolled around the cars finally seeing what he wanted, a brand new black Maserati Coupe. As he focused on the beauty of this magnificent machine, a salesperson walked up beside him.

"She a beaut," the man said.

Jake didn't answer, but instead leaned forward shading his eyes to peer inside the tinted window on the driver's door. The salesman hung back, not pressing for a sale, believing this young man was spending his day dreaming, probably just wasting the afternoon away.

Jake slowly walked around the car, inspecting it carefully.

"Want me to pop the hood and take a look?"

"Sure," Jake replied.

The engine was as shiny as the outside.

"We just got this beauty a couple of days ago, straight from the factory," he said, giving a minimal sales pitch for conversational purposes.

"Want to take her for a spin?"

Of course, he was required to be polite to those who spent money, and those who didn't.

"No, that's okay, I want to buy it," Jake answered.

"You and me both, but only in our dreams, right?" the man stated with a chuckle.

"I'm buying this car."

"Don't you want to know the price?"

"Alright, what is the cost?"

Jake realized the salesman didn't believe he could afford the car.

"I'll have to check, give me a minute. By the way, my name is John."

"John, you do that."

John walked away feeling as though he was wasting his time, but the motto was everyone was a potential customer. Jake gave another quick look at the car and followed John inside the building, and waited at the entrance. John approached from behind.

"That particular model is one-hundred and forty-five thousand dollars. Impressive, for sure."

Jake remained silent for a minute.

"I'll take it."

"Of course you will," John concurred, believing he was joking.

They both remain looking out over the lot.

"I said I want to buy that car," Jake repeated.

John turned to view his profile, unsure how to respond.

"Let's step into my office, and I'll draw up the loan papers," John said, not believing for a minute a loan would be processed.

"Cash."

"Excuse me."

"I will be paying with cash."

"Follow me."

John didn't know what to make of this, and treated Jake like any other prospective customer. He walked into his office and sat behind the desk.

"Have a seat, it takes just a minute to draw up the sales slip."

Even though John thinks a joke is being played on him, he created a legitimate document of sale on the computer, printed it out, and placed the paper down on the desk to go over the figures. He started with the list price, dealer prep fees, taxes, tag, etc explaining each line down to the bottom with the final figure. John watched him closely, waiting for the "got you" moment.

Instead, he witnessed Jake pulling out a wad of money from his pocket and began counting, laying the bills in stacks on the desk in front of him.

"Man, you were serious," John said, surprised.

Jake looked at him.

"I said I was buying that car, you didn't believe me. Maybe I shouldn't give you the commission," Jake told him, holding back a grin.

"No, no, I trusted you were serious when I saw you eyeing it."

"Right."

Though he did everything professionally, John realized this young man was no fool. He learned a lesson to not judge a book by its cover and was relieved to have not taken things for granted, for he made a hefty commission on this one.

Jake paid for the car, and John handed him the bill of sale, keys, and on a handshake Jake stood to leave, but turned in the doorway.

"By the way, find someone who can use my truck and give them a good deal."

"I will," John told him.

Jake slid onto the black leather seat, turned the key in the ignition, and listened for a minute before driving off the lot without a glance. He took his new car on the highway at full speed and pressed the radio button, adjusted the channel, and increased the volume. Now this was living, he thought.

An hour later, he returned to the hotel and flipped the keys in the air to the valet standing curbside, and walked to the elevator. He had a very busy day, and now it was time to get ready to have some fun. He was looking forward to spending the evening with a beautiful woman.

Jake was at Beverly's apartment right on time. When he knocked on the door, she came out without inviting him inside. The building she lived in wasn't anything special, like most city apartment buildings made of beige brick with an outdated architectural design.

They went to dinner at a restaurant of her choice and later to a nightclub she frequented. It was obvious to Jake that she was a party girl and enjoyed having a good time. It suited his mood, for he was in the party spirit celebrating his new life. For a weeknight, the club was crowded. They danced, drank, and were joined by some of her friends later in the evening. It turned out to be a wild night.

It was apparent to Jake, she didn't adhere to a nighttime curfew. Pushing one o'clock, he was ready to take her home. Though he enjoyed the night scene like most young people his age, he rationalized there would be plenty of opportunities for partying and had no problem pacing himself. Taking a break from dancing, they sat at a small table that held their drinks.

"Don't you have to work tomorrow?"

"Sure do."

"Shouldn't I take you home?"

Beverly took his wrist and turned it to see the watch he bought earlier.

"Looks nice on you. I suppose we should call it a night. I don't want to have raccoon eyes in the morning, it might scare off the customers," she said, tipsy.

"Right."

Jake grabbed his jacket from the back of the chair, and reached for her hand.

"Let's go."

She didn't live far from the nightclub. He pulled up alongside the curb to her apartment complex and parked.

"This was so much fun, Jake. Will I see you again?"

"Absolutely."

"Call me tomorrow."

She leaned in and kissed him on the cheek before opening her door and sliding out. Beverly turned and blew him a farewell kiss as she walked the short distance to the entrance of the building. Jake waited until she was inside the lobby before pulling out onto the street.

He enjoyed the evening with Beverly and called her for another date of dinner and dancing. She was fun to be with and liked having a good time which was exactly what he wanted also. They saw each other several evenings a week, frequenting the best restaurants and nightclubs in the city. Often, her friends would join them for drinking and dancing. This was the life he always dreamt of and could finally live it openly without criticism. Jake felt he had been released from a lifelong sentence of drudgery.

Jake spent his days becoming acquainted with the city while living in the Lincoln Plaza Hotel. The next thing he needed to do was find a permanent place to live, but wasn't interested in a house, too much upkeep. A condominium suited him.

Wherever he traveled, Jake took his laptop and spent time throughout the day to study the specific money market websites he monitored. He was being cautious having yet to make an investment, for he wasn't a spontaneous investor. He had already spent a sizable amount of money and knew it wouldn't last if he kept to this pace, but was confident to make it up soon.

Chapter 8

After a month of living in the city, Jake walked into a swanky restaurant near the downtown area and is seated at a table with a high-back bench seat in dark gray fabric and white-clothed round table. The establishment reflected elegance with chandelier lighting and subtle decor in a black and white theme. He ordered a drink and as he sipped the cocktail, two attractive women came to his table.

"Is there anything we can get you, sir?" the tall, dark-haired woman asked.

"Like what?"

"Whatever would make you happy," the second woman replied.

Jake was surprised to be approached by two women, and wondered if they were part of the management, treating all patrons this way. He decided to play along.

"There is something you can do, join me for a drink."

The two women glanced at each other and quickly sat on either side of Jake.

"I guess that's my answer."

"What's your name?" the dark-haired woman asked.

"I'm Jake, and you are?"

"I'm Elise and this is Robin," Elise said.

"It's nice to meet you both."

The women were in their mid-twenties and apparently looking for a good time. Jake motioned a waitress to his table, ordered a bottle of wine, and she returned with one of their best Cabernet Sauvignon's and three glasses.

Jake was enjoying the company listening to the women talk about their acting careers, and the trials of going on numerous auditions. As they chatted, an attractive petite blonde sitting across the room caught his attention with her infectious smile exposing perfect white teeth. He remained infatuated as she conversed with her friends. Jake surmised she was older by several years, probably in her late thirties, but he was fascinated with her seemingly natural charisma. Inquisitive, he asked.

"Who's that blonde over there?"

Elise turned to see who he was referring to.

"Oh, that's Laura Denton, she's an actress too."

"Really."

"In fact, we've worked together on a movie called, 'A Box for Rob'."

"Who's the man that just walked up to her?"

"That's Frank D'Maggio. He owns this restaurant."

Frank had the typical stature of a business man in a black suit perfectly matched to his well trimmed black hair. Even wearing an eye patch over his left eye didn't distract from his masculine appearance.

Frank noticed Jake watching them, and left Laura to check on a new customer.

"Hello, Elise, good to see you again," Frank told her.

Elise made the introductions.

"This is Frank D'Maggio, the owner of this establishment, this is Jake."

"Jake, pleasure to meet you."

"Frank," Jake said, reaching out to shake his hand.

"Enjoying yourself."

"We are," Jake replied.

"Well, you should be, you have lovely company. If I can get you anything, let me know."

"Will do."

"Maria, cover this table," Frank said to a nearby waitress, before stepping away.

Jake returned his attention to Laura.

"So, an actress."

"You really like her," Elise told him.

He didn't answer.

"Yes, it's obvious."

Avoiding her comment, Jake placed a toast.

"Cheers ladies, to a great night."

"Drink up, we'll need another bottle," Robin interjected.

Maria took their order for the evening meal. Jake realized the women in his company were expecting him to fund for their dinner also. A second bottle of wine was brought to the table, and Jake is barely keeping up with the conversation, so riveted with Laura. Three steaks were delivered and while they ate, Elise and Robin were in constant conversation about things that didn't interest Jake.

Laura was aware of capturing the attention of an admirer and relying on her acting skills, she left her friends and went to sit at the bar, isolating herself for his approach. Jake paid the hefty tab and politely excused himself to follow her, taking the seat next to Laura.

"Can I buy you a drink?" he asked, motioning the bartender.

"Do I know you?"

"Not yet, I'm Jake."

"Laura," she said, extending her hand to shake his.

"What will you have?" the bartender asked.

"Joe, give me a vodka-on-the-rocks."

"Make it two," Jake said.

She focused her attention back on Jake.

"Are you new to the city?"

"Been here a month."

"What do you do?"

"I do a lot of things."

Laura is very direct, not wasting time with unnecessary verbal foreplay.

"Okay, how about your job?"

"I'm an investor."

"Stock market?"

"Amongst other ventures, yes."

"Are you any good?"

Their conversation was interrupted when the bartender requested Jake pay for their drinks. He pulled out a role of hundred dollar bills, and paid the bartender with one of them. Laura noticed the cash. She directed another question at him.

"Where do you live?"

"Nowhere, yet," he replied, shoving the money back into his pocket.

"I've been staying at the Lincoln Plaza."

"Nice."

"Why, do you know of anywhere decent?"

"Do you have a pen?"

Jake saw one on the counter and handed it to her, and Laura wrote on a napkin.

"There is a condo for sale in the building where I live."

"Your building, wow, that's a leap of faith, don't you think. I could be a serial killer."

She looked at him.

"So could I," Laura replied with a smile.

She handed him the napkin with the address and property manager's phone number. Jake folded it, and placed it in his jacket pocket. He was so enthralled with her, he wasn't observant to the nature of her questions.

"So, I hear you are an actress."

"What have you heard?"

"Just that. Have you been in anything I might have seen?"

"Probably not, but I will be."

Frank stepped up behind Laura, and leaned in to whisper.

"Got to go."

She smiled at Jake and stood up.

"Bye, Jake, nice to meet you," she said.

"Good night, Jake," Frank said, leaving him alone at the bar.

Jake nodded his head watching them leave the restaurant together and wondered about their relationship. Though there wasn't a ring on her finger, he didn't know if she was his wife, or girlfriend, but planned to find out. There was something about her that intrigued him, and definitely wanted to get to know her better.

Chapter 9

William had not heard from Jake, and hoped he would have phoned home by now. He tried to call his cellphone once, but Jake didn't answer. He had no way of knowing where he was, but William made no further attempt to reach him. He knew it was the way Jake wanted it.

A longtime friend, Sid Rothenberg, stopped by the house to visit William. He was tall and slender with white hair and lightly tanned skin. Sid's nickname for his friend was Abe, a spinoff of William's last name. Sid entered the office to be greeted by Mrs. Grey.

"Why Mr. Rothenberg, what brings you out this way?"

"Came to see my friend."

"Your timing is good. He's in his office, go on in."

"How are you doing?" he asked.

"Can't complain and if I did, it wouldn't do me any good," she told him with humor.

"I'm sure you know where the best place to send complaints to," he said, countering.

"That I do."

Sid walked over to William's door, and tapped on it before entering. William looked up from his paperwork and stood, reaching across his desk to shake Sid's hand.

"Sid, what brings you by?"

"Wanted to see how you were holding up. Any word from Jake?" he asked, getting to the reason for his visit.

William had phoned him of Jake's leaving home.

"No, nothing. I tried calling him once, but he didn't answer his cellphone. I'm worried he may be going down the wrong path."

"Trust God, Abe. You know at Passover, we were instructed to smear the blood of a lamb on the doorpost, but what most people miss is that blood was for the whole family, trust God."

"I'm trying to do just that, but it's still hard."

"As a father, you have the right to be concerned for your son. I've known you for years, Abe, and you did the right thing to cut him loose. He's a grown man finding his way in this world. You couldn't have held him back, he would have left anyway."

"That's true."

"He'll be back one day," Sid told him.

"Not soon enough."

"You never left the farm, nor your father, or his father. I can see Seth is following in your footsteps. Whatever the reason that Jake feels compelled to leave, he'll return when he's ready, make no mistake about that."

"I hope you're right."

"Think of it this way. As God's children, we may stray from His hedge of protection, but even so, we are unconditionally loved and forgiven. The same holds true of Jacob, he just doesn't know it yet. God's love and yours will sustain him. I assure you, he'll come home."

"Thanks, Sid. I needed to hear that right now."

"Then there was a reason for my coming out to see you this morning. I'll be on my way, let me know if you hear from him."

"I appreciate you stopping by."

He followed Sid out of the office, and walked with him outside. They stood on the porch watching Seth coming towards them.

"Hello, Sid," Seth said, greeting their family friend.

"Seth, how are you these days?"

"Swamped with work. Jake leaves at the busiest time of the season, figures."

"A man has to do what he has to do, can't hold that against him," Sid said.

"He could've picked a better time to do his disappearing act. Never mind, it doesn't matter."

"Are you saying you would rather he be here helping on the farm."

"No, better he's gone. I can do the work for both of us."

On that note, Seth walked away, not wanting to discuss Jake any longer. William watched him go into the office.

"Well, my friend, I'll talk to you soon. Hold your faith."

William didn't respond to Sid's final words. They shook hands, and he waited until Sid drove away to walk over to the barn. Seeing there was work to be done, he went to the bin filtering kernels of husked corn and began helping alongside the men. Now wasn't the time to dwell on his youngest, but later he would speak to God about him. Seth walked into the barn about an hour later to find his father working. William stepped away.

"What is it, Seth? Got a problem?"

"Nothing I can't handle. Why was Sid out this way?"

"Came to see how I was doing since Jake left."

Seth looked away for a moment before speaking.

"I don't get it. He was seldom here and when he was, he didn't work, and yet, everyone is talking about him like he's someone special."

"He is special, and so are you. Apparently, your brother wanted something this farm couldn't give him. The opportunity is for you also, if you want a life other than farming."

"You know this farm is all that matters, and there is nothing beyond these fields that interest me."

"Then try to accept that Jake doesn't feel the same way you, or I do about this business."

"He thinks he can make it big in the city, but I have my doubts," Seth told him.

"I suppose in time, we'll find out."

"I've got to get back to work, see you at dinner," Seth said.

He didn't want to talk about Jake.

William went to his office. He still had a pile of paperwork to get through before the end of the day. They were picking up two new vendors, and he needed to go over the applications and have Mrs. Grey set up their accounts. Something he realized Jake would be doing if he were here. Whether Jake was present or not, the work had to be done.

Chapter 10

The following morning with Laura's reference, Jake placed a call to the number written on the napkin. It was the property manager, Strutton and Associates, of the condominium complex she recommended.

"Hello, I was told to give your office a call regarding a condo unit you have available at The Plaza Residences."

"Yes, we have three units. Two are for sale, and one is a fully furnished rental with option to purchase. Would you be interested in seeing them?" the young woman asked.

"Yes, is it possible to see them today?"

"I can meet you in the lobby at eleven o'clock. Will that work for you?"

"It will."

"Who am I speaking with?"

"My name is Jake Abraham."

"Jake, I'm Sandra Anderson, and I look forward to meeting you later this morning. I assume you know how to get to the complex."

"I'll find it."

With two hours till he met with Sandra, Jake went to a nearby cafe for breakfast and spent the morning focused on the stock market from his laptop. He arrived at the complex minutes before Sandra made an appearance. The Plaza Residences was on the outskirts of the downtown area in an exclusive area. The building was imposing, located off the main road with its towering golden-colored brick exterior and black window shutters with matching wrought-iron balconies.

Jake parked his car in front and stood for a moment looking upwards at the building. On either side were other apartment complexes, but not as architecturally attractive as this one. He walked inside the double-glassed doors to the main lobby with stainless steel elevators across opposing walls. He heard the door open from behind and turned to see an attractive woman he guessed to be in her mid-thirties with long blonde hair and blue eyes. Sandra approached extending her hand to shake his.

"Hi, you must be Jake."

"Yes."

"Nice to meet you, I'm Sandra. Before I show you the units, tell me what are you looking for in amenities. How many bedrooms, baths, things like that?"

"Maybe three bedrooms."

"Is this for you, or a family? How many people will be living in the condo?"

"Just myself."

"A bachelor pad is what you are looking for."

"If living single is what you call it, then yes."

"I'll show you all three, but I think I know the one that will interest you. We'll look at the two unfurnished first. Do you have your own furniture?"

"No, furnished would be great."

"Before we take the tour, I'll give you a quick history of the complex. This building is six years old, so it has all the latest amenities such as marbled countertops, stainless steel appliances, hard wood floors, recessed light fixtures, ceiling fans, but you'll see all that for yourself in a minute. Most of the residents own and live in their units, except for a few that are investment properties. The unit I think you will be most interested in was bought for that purpose; however, they are now wanting to sell it. There are forty-five units on nine floors, and they are not all the same square footage, or floor plan."

"Let's take the elevator, and you can see if anything interests you," she continued.

"Sounds good."

They went to the fifth floor looking at one of the unfurnished units, and then to the sixth to view the other empty apartment. The furnished condo was on the seventh floor and a corner unit. The moment Jake walked inside, he was awestruck. The simple earthen decor suited his style. It was very spacious and appealing with tan leather sofa and matching chairs, stone and glass encased tables and one wall done in beige stone. He held his comments walking further into the open living area and then into the master bedroom, two additional bedrooms, and glanced in the bathrooms before backtracking to the modern kitchen.

Sandra waited patiently near the kitchen counter letting him explore on his own. When he finished his observation, he walked up to her.

"This unit is twenty-one hundred square feet, three bedroom, two baths, with a beautiful balcony overlooking the garden and pond in the back of the complex."

Jake went to the window and pulled back the blinds of the oversized sliding glass door. He walked out onto the balcony and looked down.

"What do you think?" Sandra asked from behind.

"Very nice. How much is it?"

"The owner wants to sell at four hundred and seventy-five thousand, but is willing to lease for one year on a purchase agreement."

"If I decide to buy, what is required for the down payment and monthly rental?"

"Let's go back inside, and I'll get my calculator."

She locked the door behind her, and they went to the kitchen counter.

"They want half up front as the deposit, and the remaining balance can be divided into twelve monthly increments."

Sandra punched some numbers.

"Two hundred thirty-seven thousand dollars as the down payment with a monthly rental fee of approximately twenty-thousand. At the end of the year, additional closing costs would be added such as title transfer, taxes, insurance, association fee, etc.," she explained.

Jake took another walk around the apartment accessing the figures in his head. Feeling confident he could gain the deposit back with solid investments, he agreed.

"I'll take it."

"Great. If you'll follow me to my office, I can process the loan application and the sooner we get an approval from the mortgage company, the quicker you can take possession."

"I'll be paying with cash," Jake informed her.

Sandra looked at this young man in front of her, and wondered how he could have that large amount of money.

"You know, I never asked what you did for a living," she inquired.

"I'm an investor."

"What kind of investor? Do you mean mutual funds, stocks, bonds, things like that?"

"Exactly."

"You must be very good at it to pay cash for this condo."

"I'm working on it."

"I still need you to follow me to the office for the necessary paperwork. Are you free now?"

"Sure, I want to move in this afternoon, if possible."

"That shouldn't be a problem since you are purchasing with cash."

They left the building, and he walked Sandra to her car.

"Where are you parked?"

"That black one over there," Jake said, pointing to his car three down from hers.

"I'm impressed."

Jake left her standing at her car making his way towards his own vehicle. She pulled into traffic and he followed the ten minute drive to her office, a small place nestled in a strip mall with other businesses. The storefronts were identical in beige and gray brick with large windows and glass doors.

They walked to a back office, and Sandra settled at her desk and began typing on the computer's keyboard while Jake sat patiently.

"Much of the paperwork can be omitted since we aren't processing a loan application, but I still need to acquire the basic information."

"I understand."

Within thirty minutes, she printed the necessary documents and began explaining each one carefully. First, the Purchase and Sales Agreement with the Real Estate Purchase Addendum reflecting the rental part of the contract. She explained the total cost, minus closing expenses, the down payment, and the monthly rental fee, and that payments are made to her firm, Strutton and Associates Property Management.

"Once you make the down payment, I'll release the keys. The first month's rent isn't due for thirty days from the date on the contract, and you can take possession of your new home," she informed him.

"I'll have the money in a couple of hours."

"If you'll back here by three, I can make the deposit before the end of the day."

"Not a problem."

Sandra reached across the desk to shake Jake's hand.

"It's a pleasure doing business with you, Mr. Abraham."

Jake nodded and left her office. To be called Mr. Abraham reminded him of his father, and he didn't want to think about his family. They weren't a part of this new life he was carving out for himself. He shrugged his shoulders and walked out of the building towards his shiny Maserati, instantly forgetting his roots.

Jake returned to Strutton and Associates with the down payment. Sandra looked up from her desk when she saw him standing in the doorway.

"I'm ready to sign those papers."

Sandra reached behind her for the folder on the credenza. She opened the file and removed the documents explaining again the purchase price, terms of agreement, and proposed closing costs, and reiterated the net balance will be due in one year.

"Looks to be in order, where do I sign?"

She handed him a pen, pointing to each line that required his signature. Jake took his cash and began counting two hundred and thirty-seven thousand dollars. She watched, not expecting to see so much money.

"I didn't realize you brought cash, I was thinking a bank check."

Jake stopped counting and looked at her.

"Didn't cross my mind, this is easier."

He had to gather the stacks of money and start his count again. This time she didn't interrupt and when he was finished, she gathered each pile separately and recounted to confirm the amount. She placed the money in a large bank envelope, and locked it in her desk drawer. Next, she made a copy of the documents, slipped them into a folder, and handed it to Jake.

"These are your copies, along with your receipt for the down payment, and the keys. Congratulations on your purchase," she said, handing them to him.

"That was easy enough."

"Yes, it was and I thank you for your business. If there is anything else I can do, please let me know."

"I will, thank you."

Jake stood and they shook hands.

"Enjoy your new home."

"I intend to."

He left her office satisfied with the purchase. Jake checked out of the hotel with his possessions stashed in the car and was now driving to the complex. With his small suitcase, duffel bag hanging over his left shoulder and balancing an arm full of new clothing on hangers, he walked into the condo heading for the master bedroom. After throwing the duffel bag on the bed and hanging the clothes in the walk-in closet, Jake is surprised to hear a knock at the door. Laura was standing in the hallway.

"Hello, neighbor, I see you got the condo," she said.

"How did you know I was here?"

"Oh, a little birdie told me. Can I come in?"

He opened the door wider, and Laura walked into the living room area and looked around.

"Very nice, I haven't been in this particular unit."

She turned around to face Jake.

"I like the decor, suits you."

"I still don't understand how you knew I was here," he said, pressing the point.

"It's no secret, Sandra is my friend."

Now it made sense.

"Of course, pushing some business her way. I'm sure she made a hefty commission today."

"She did, and we're celebrating at Frank's restaurant this evening. Why don't you join us? That is unless you have something more important to do," she said, flirting with him.

"No, I think I can manage. What time?"

"I live on the fourth floor, 415. Pick me up at six."

"Okay, I'll see you then."

Laura walked passed him towards the door with Jake following behind. She turned just outside the entrance.

"By the way, now you owe me, big...big...big."

"I didn't realize that."

"Huge," she said, teasingly, before walking to the elevator.

"Bye," Jake said, grinning.

He closed the door and returned to the bedroom to retrieve his laptop from the duffel bag, and sat on the sofa propping it on his lap to study the market.

"Time to make some money," he said aloud, rubbing his hands together.

He spent the next two hours focused on two company's stock waiting to see how they trended. Patience was an important factor in buying and selling, and right now, he was in the waiting mode.

Realizing he was hungry, Jake placed the computer on the sofa and went into the kitchen to look for food, even though he didn't expect to find any. He left the condo to stock up on a few items at the nearest grocery store.

When he returned, he rechecked his sites and noticed that one of the company's stock value had changed. He transferred money from an account he had established while in college used strictly for this purpose, and decided to invest conservatively. He shut down the computer to get ready for an evening with Laura and Sandra.

Chapter 11

Jake stood outside Laura's apartment door at six sharp. She answered but didn't invite him in.

"I see you are a punctual person."

"Not always."

They walked towards the elevator.

"We're going to have a great time this evening."

"I was hoping for that."

"Let's take your car. Frank will bring me home, if you want to leave early."

"Alright."

Jake opened the passenger door, and Laura slid onto the seat. He walked around the front of the car and got behind the wheel.

"I love that fresh leather smell, don't you?"

"That I do."

He steered out of the complex parking lot into evening traffic.

"What's the deal with you and Frank?" Jake asked, glancing in her direction.

"Frank and I go way back. He was one of the first people I met when I moved to this city."

"How long have you been here?"

"Ten years."

"Really, what brought you here?"

"Acting. I've traveled around and lived in different places, but when I came here and met Frank, we connected, so I stayed."

"Are you two married?"

Laura looked at his profile and laughed.

"No, just good friends."

"You know what I do for a living, but what do you do when you aren't acting?" he inquired, curious.

"When I'm not doing a commercial or a short-film, I go on auditions and wait until something comes along. I really want to be in a feature film. That would be my big break in the industry," she told him.

"How's that?"

"I would be accepted as a legitimate actor, could even become famous."

It didn't take long to drive to Frank's Restaurant and Bar on the north end of town. After finding a spot near the front entrance, Jake parked and helped Laura with her door. Together they walked into the darkened building. The hostess recognized Laura.

"Good evening, Laura," she said.

"Hello, Bonnie. Need a table for three, something private."

"Absolutely. Follow me, please."

Laura walked behind Bonnie with Jake following.

"We're expecting my friend, Sandra. Will you show her to our table when she arrives?"

"Of course."

A waitress came over to the table offering them wine.

"Maybe later, I'll take a gin and tonic. Jake, what about you?"

"Scotch-on-the-rocks."

"I'll be right back with your drinks. Laura, shall I let Frank know you're here?"

"Sure, he's expecting us."

"Everyone seems to know you," Jake commented.

He wasn't sure why, but it made him uncomfortable.

"I hang out here often. It's a great place to meet people; after all, I met you," she said, flirting.

"Right."

He wanted to establish her relationship with Frank.

"Do the employees think you and Frank are a couple?"

"They see us together, but we don't flaunt our friendship. Why, does that bother you?"

"I'm not sure, maybe."

"Don't worry about Frank," she said, reassuring him.

Before he could respond, the drinks arrive. While sipping on his, Frank made an appearance.

"Laura, you're looking lovely."

"Thank you," she replied, tilting her head slightly.

"Is anyone joining you this evening?"

"Yes, my friend, Sandra. Jake bought a condo in my building, so we're celebrating his purchase and Sandra's commission."

"That is worth celebrating."

Jake listened to the conversation, and there was something about their relationship that disturbed him. Their speech was very formal for friends, somewhat rehearsed, he thought.

Sandra joined them.

"Hello, Frank."

"Sandra, it's always good to see you."

Everyone seemed very familiar with Frank's establishment, Jake realized.

"Sonia will take care of you. I've got to get back to work, but enjoy yourselves."

"We will," Laura replied.

"Jake, my friend, you're in the company of two of my favorite people. Have a pleasant evening."

Jake nodded.

Jake ordered prime rib, while both Laura and Sandra opted for lobster. Complimentary wine was brought to the table and long after the meal was finished, they talked and drank into the late evening hour. Jake enjoyed listening to Laura and Sandra's bantering, comparing acting gigs to the real estate business, keeping the conversation lively.

"Jake, are you feeling okay?" Laura asked, noticing he looked pale.

"I need to call it a night. Are you ready to leave?"

"No, it's still early for me, but you go ahead. Frank can take me home."

"Are you sure?"

"Not a problem."

He paid the check surprised to see it was nearly two hundred dollars, and left them sitting at the table. Laura and Sandra watched him.

"He seems like a nice young man," Sandra stated.

"I think he has a crush on me."

"No kidding, isn't he a bit young for you, and besides, what would Frank say?"

"Frank isn't my guardian. I can see whoever I want. Anyway, I'm hoping to connect him with Frank on a business deal."

"Really."

"The way he spends money, and have you seen the car he drives?"

"I have."

"That's no cheap car," Laura said, pondering the matter.

"Well, you and Frank seem to rub each other's back."

"We take care of each other, if that's what you mean."

"That's what I mean," Sandra confirmed, before taking a sip of her drink.

"By the way, thanks for the referral."

"My pleasure, that's what friends are for," Laura said, lifting her glass for a toast.

They click their glasses and smiled in understanding.

Jake enjoyed his time with Laura and Sandra but was eager to get back to the condo and check his most recent investment. He needed to seriously begin making money, or else his inheritance would disappear far too quickly having already spent a sizable amount since arriving in the city.

Chapter 12

Frank took Laura home that evening, something he was accustomed to. Unbeknown to Jake, the condominium she lived in belonged to Frank, as she revealed only a half-truth about her relationship with him. He took an interest in a beautiful but broke actress years ago, and kept her under his wing. Young and desperate, Laura accepted his invitation, and they've been together ever since.

She had a talent for persuading men to make business investments that otherwise may not have transpired. Frank was a wealthy man, she a needy woman, and it made for a perfect arrangement. Her monetary rewards were many including the condo, clothing, jewelry, and a convertible sports car. Acting was her calling card and the excuse given for being professionally unemployed. It was plausible and acceptable in the group of people she hung around.

Laura spent her evenings at the restaurant in full acting persona scouting the patrons carefully. It wasn't hard to detect Jake the first night he was there, for she saw him watching her. She always liked the adrenaline rush she felt when meeting someone for the first time, anticipating the outcome. Walking into the condo later that night, she immediately took off her high-heeled shoes and threw her cashmere coat on the sofa.

"What an evening," Laura commented.

"You've been very busy these past couple of days," Frank replied.

"Yes, I have."

Unlike Jake's apartment with its earthen tones and muted colors, her unit was vibrant shades of green, orange and yellow, very contemporary and artsy. They sat close together on the bright green overstuffed sofa, and he placed his hand on her knee.

"It was a good move to help Sandra."

"She was needing some cash. Sales were down, and besides Jake was looking for a place. It seemed perfect for both of them."

"Indeed."

"That was a stellar performance, but then I always knew you were a good actress," he told her, gently squeezing her knee.

"Did you have any doubt?"

"Never."

Frank leaned in and kissed her.

"Just don't forget you're mine."

"I could never forget that."

"Make sure you don't."

She kissed him back.

"Are you jealous?"

"I don't get jealous."

"He's a boy, and a very rich one it appears," she reminded him.

"Do what you do best."

"Don't I always?"

"We're a good team, you and I," he told her.

"Of course."

"It's late, let's go to bed," he said.

Frank extended his hand to Laura, and they walked arm in arm to the bedroom. Early the next morning, Laura answered her door to see Jake standing there.

"Jake, I didn't expect to see you this morning. What brings you by?"

Jake is stumped for what to say, now that he's at her door.

"I came to borrow some eggs."

"Excuse me."

"Some neighbors borrow eggs from each other, from time to time," he said, stumbling with his words.

"When do I get them back?" Laura asked, playing along.

Jake looked puzzled.

"The eggs because you are borrowing them," she said, seeing his confusion.

"I confess, I just wanted an excuse to see you."

"You need an excuse to see me."

"Do you want to have dinner with me?" he asked.

"Of course, she'll have dinner with you," Frank answered, walking up behind Laura.

He passed between them in the doorway.

"Welcome to the neighborhood, Jake," Frank said, patting him on the back as he headed for the elevator.

Frank turned and spoke to Jake.

"Pal, you'd better get a better game on, that line is weak. Happy scrambling."

"Yeah," Jake replied, disturbed by his presence.

"Take care, Babe."

"So, do you want those eggs? How many, two, three, a dozen?" Laura asked, opening the door wider as Jake followed her into the kitchen.

"What is Frank doing here?"

"Business," she replied.

"At seven-thirty in the morning."

"You're here at seven-thirty."

"Now that you mention it, it probably is too early."

"Want some coffee?" she asked, reaching for two cups.

"Sure."

"Did you really come by to ask me to dinner?"

"Yes, and to see if you want to spend the day together."

She poured the coffee and handed one to Jake, pointing to the cream and sugar on the counter.

"I thought maybe we could take in some of the sights, since you've lived here awhile. That's if you aren't busy."

"I'd enjoy that, but I can't today. I have some things to take care of, but we could plan for another day."

"No problem, I shouldn't have bothered you this morning."

"Can we do it later in the week?"

"You know where I live, so whenever it's convenient for you. It was just an idea."

"There are several wonderful things to see in Springfield. Let me get back to you."

"That's why I was hoping for a tour. I should go, thanks for the coffee."

"Anytime, Jake, we're neighbors."

He walked to the door, and opened it to leave.

"I'll be in touch," she told him.

Jake walked to the elevator and pushed the button to the seventh floor. He wondered what kind of business Frank had that brought him to Laura's apartment so early. His mind drifted to the obvious. Since Frank took her home last night, did he spend the night? Perhaps, he lived with her, otherwise, why would he welcome him to the neighborhood, that seemed strange, he thought. He didn't know what their involvement with each other might entail, but he was getting the feeling there was more then she willingly admitted. He wasn't sure how he felt about it.

Later that evening, Jake stayed in his apartment focused on researching sites to consider for investments, but his attention was periodically drawn to the television, and he stopped working to listen.

Chapter 13

Jake left the complex to walk the area and stopped at a quaint coffee shop four blocks from his apartment. It was called Siesta Cafe and very convenient, he realized. He went inside to stand in line while studying the menu board posted on the wall behind the counter. The establishment was busy, and he was still indecisive when his turn to order.

"Having a hard time figuring out what you want?" the young girl behind the counter asked.

"Yes, my first time in here."

"What are you in the mood for?"

"I don't know, something with a little style."

"What about a Raspberry Mocha?"

"That sounds stylish. No, make it an Expresso Romano."

"One expresso coming up."

She rang up the order.

"Do you live nearby, or just passing through?"

"I bought a place a few of blocks down at the Plaza Residences," he said, reaching inside his pocket for money.

"The whole building?" she asked, teasingly.

"No, just one condo."

"That will be four-fifty."

Jake handed her a hundred dollar bill, and she held it in the air.

"Do you need change?" she asked, knowingly.

"Sorry, I don't have anything smaller. Can you break it?"

"That's fine."

She sidestepped to the register to get his change.

"Do you have wi-fi here?"

"Sure do, here's the password."

She handed him a card with a number on it.

"Here is your change, Mr. Trump," she said, flirting.

"Donald's just an alias, my friends call me Jake."

"If any of those friends come in, I'll have them escorted to your table. I'm Summer, let me know if you need anything else."

"Summer. Any particular reason why you are named a season?" Jake inquired.

"I was born in the summertime."

"Not very creative of your parents."

"Don't you like my name?"

"It's cute, what's your last name?"

"Fellows. Summer Marie Fellows, to be exact."

"Well, Summer Marie Fellows, it's nice to meet you."

"What is yours?"

"I'm Jacob Abraham."

"Wow, Jacob and Abraham, two important biblical names. Which one do you favor?" she asked, pointedly.

"Neither, I'm not like either one."

"Really, why do you say that?"

"For starters, I don't have the kind of relationship with God that Jacob or Abraham did."

"I bet you could if you tried."

"How did we get onto this subject?"

"Your name."

"Right, call me Jake."

Jake did not want to get into a discussion about God.

"Good to meet you, Summertime. I'll be coming in here more often."

She laughed seeing he could give as easily as he got.

"I hope you do."

He sat at the counter and took his laptop from the backpack he had stuffed in his duffel bag when he left home, and sat it on the counter. Summer placed the hot expresso carefully beside it.

"Here you go, Mr. Trump."

Jake glanced up and smiled at her.

"Thanks, Summer in the City."

She laughed, knowing the song.

Briefly, he watched her working behind the counter. She was young and cute with her slim stature, long auburn hair, and brown eyes. His attention is quickly redirected to the investment site as he studied the charts and numbers from yesterday's investment. He sat for an hour punching keys on the laptop while the coffee turned cold. Summer kept an eye on him as she continued to greet customers and prepare drinks. She walked over to him.

"Would you like a fresh expresso? I think this one has gotten cold; no charge."

"That would be great."

She took his cup and replaced it with another coffee without disturbing him. She could tell he was in deep concentration. He leaned back entwining his fingers together, and rested the back of his head still focused on the monitor. Summer couldn't resist talking with him.

"What are you working on? You've been involved in your computer for nearly two hours."

"I study the stock market," he said, nonchalantly.

"Really, what do you do?"

"There are specific companies that I follow their trends," he told her, giving the short explanation.

"Do you actually invest money?"

"I do. That's the whole idea; buy stock and sell stock to make money."

"What happens if you buy, and you lose money?"

"That's the beauty of it, got to know when to invest and when not to."

"You must be good."

"I work at it. Just like now, the stock I bought yesterday has just increased, and I made some money."

"Do you keep investing in the same stock?"

"Not always, there are several companies I follow."

"Sounds to me like gambling because you never know what could happen."

Jake didn't care for the terminology and was finished with the direction the conversation was taking. He closed the computer and put it in his backpack.

"Got to go."

"See you around."

She watched him walk out of the cafe wondering if she said something to offend him. Jake went back to the condo to work without interruption, and within the next few hours, he made another decision to move more money from his account. It was always a tricky proposition, but he didn't see it as gambling. He did his research and knew what he was doing.

Chapter 14

William and Seth stood outside. For a moment, neither spoke and surveyed the condition of the land.

"We haven't had a drop of rain in a month," Seth said.

"I know."

"If we don't get some rain, next year's crop will be sparse," he continued.

"We'll give it a few more days, but may have to bring out the water tanks," William told him.

"I hope we don't have to resort to that. I'm going out to the barn."

"I've got some paperwork."

Seth walked away while William went to the office.

"Sam's in your office," Mrs. Grey told him when he came through the door.

Heavy-hearted for what he was about to do, William walked in and took a seat behind his desk.

"Maggie said you wanted to see me."

He was the only one who called her by her first name.

"I have some unfortunate news. We're having to cut back, and the foreman position is one of those areas."

Sam is stunned.

"What are you saying? Am I being let go?"

"It's a tough decision, and this drought isn't helping matters. When things pick up again, we certainly want you back. I'm sorry, Sam."

"I always thought the business was doing well. What has brought on such a drastic change?"

"As you know, production has slowed considerably, and we need all the cash we can hold onto. I don't see a choice but to cut your salary just as we have other expenses."

William hated to fire Sam because he had been with them for a long time, but it wasn't just him, nearly half of the men wouldn't be returning. He and Seth would have to do the work.

"We'll take care of you, Sam. We have a good severance package. You should find something long before the money runs out."

"I appreciate the severance, but I can't believe you're firing me," he said, shaking his head.

"It's going to work out," William told him.

"How is it going to work out when this is the only job I've ever had? I started here right out of college, and truthfully, I don't want to work anywhere else."

"Tell you what, Sam, give me a few weeks and let's see what happens. The severance should help, and I'll be in touch."

William walked around his desk. Sam stood up, and William initiated an embrace and handshake.

"It's been an honor to work for you."

"It's been my honor too, Sam. I'm really sorry about this, but don't lose faith."

Sam walked out of the office without a glance towards Mrs. Grey. William followed him to the front door with Seth passing Samuel in the doorway.

"What's wrong with Sam? He looked upset," Seth asked.

"I had to let him go."

"What? Not Sam; are we that bad off?"

"We're producing half as much as we usually do."

They went into William's office.

"Sam has been with us for years. He's like one of the family, and you won't find a more dedicated person."

"I know that, but we simply can't afford his salary."

"I wish you'd discussed this with me," Seth said, disappointed.

"What difference would it have made. In the end, he would still lose his job. We'll be cutting back on the hired help too."

"When did it get to this point? We have to do something."

"I realize that, but unless we get some rain and recover our crops, we'll have to function on a strict budget because production is down."

Seth looked at his father, upset that he wasn't consulted. He'd never fire Sam. Seth left the office. Lately, nothing seemed to be going right. Mrs. Grey appeared in the doorway, and William lifted his head when he sensed her presence.

"What is it? Another problem."

"No, I just feel bad for Sam."

"So do I, I never wanted to do that."

"I'm sure he understands, but still, he has to find another job, and they aren't easy to come by these days."

"Are you trying to make me feel worse?"

"No, I should've kept my mouth shut, sorry."

She turned and walked back to her desk, and William stayed in the office the remainder of the afternoon. Mrs. Grey left at her usual time of five o'clock with a brief wave before leaving. Best to not say anything more, she didn't want to be next.

Chapter 15

Jake returned to the Siesta Cafe a few days later and went to a table in the back corner, pulled out his laptop and a pair of earphones. Summer spotted him.

"Welcome back, I wasn't sure you would return."

"Why not?"

"I thought I said something to offend you."

"What might that be?"

"You know, when I said what you did was gambling. I didn't mean any disrespect to you, or what you do for a living," she explained.

"No harm done, maybe to some it might seem that way, but not if you know what you're doing."

"Well, I'm sorry for what I said."

Jake saw her earnest expression.

"Forgotten."

"Good, what would you like to drink?"

"Just coffee with cream."

"Coming right up."

He placed earphones in his ears.

"You know, we have live music," she pointed out.

"Sorry, did you say something?"

"I said, we have live music."

Jake turned to see the woman with a guitar at a small makeshift stage to the left of the entrance.

"Right."

"The singers are here to be heard."

"I see how this might look bad, but I wasn't listening to music."

She walked away returning with a cup of coffee, and carefully set it on the table away from the laptop.

"Can I get you anything else? Would you like a cinnamon bun to go with your coffee?"

"No thanks, just the coffee."

Summer leaned in to see what he is doing, and quizzed him.

"What are you playing?"

"I'm not playing anything. I'm studying a company that makes video games."

"What is there to study about a video game?"

"I'm researching the manufacturer."

"What, video violence on impressionable minds?"

He looked at her.

"I'm sure I passed impressionable a few years ago. This is a company I bought stock in, and apparently they make millions on these games."

"Video games?"

"Yes, I study their market trend. This particular one is a beta version that will be in the stores next week."

"Do you think it will to be a big hit?"

"I think it will make over two hundred million in sales in the first week."

Glancing around to make sure all the customers were served, Summer sat down at the table.

"So you make money off your money on other people's projects," she said, trying to understand.

"Exactly."

"Must be nice when you win."

"It is."

"This is what you do all day?"

"It's my work. I've already bought a thousand shares in this company."

"What if you lose it?"

"I don't see that happening. You have to do your homework and research potential investments thoroughly."

"Have you ever lost money?"

"Everyone loses sometimes, it goes with the territory, but I will say, my losses haven't been significant enough to break the bank."

"Okay, say this big investment goes bad, what do you do?"

Jake was uneasy with her line of questioning.

"What's with the twenty questions?"

"Sorry, it's none of my business."

"It's not going to happen, I know what I'm doing," he said, defensively.

"You don't have control over it, and it is a risk."

"There is some inherit risk, but worst case scenario, I break even or lose some cash in the short term if the game doesn't sell, but I'm not going to lose."

Attempting to lighten the conversation, Summer offered a wager.

"You're on. If you're right, free Romano's for a month."

"If I'm wrong?"

"Then you have to get a real job bussing tables right here."

"A real job, really. You don't see what I do as work. Just because I'm not doing a nine to five schedule, doesn't mean that my method of earning a living is any less productive than yours. I simply do it in a different way."

"It's not a steady paycheck. I'm not questioning your ability, but you have no control on the outcome."

"I've got this covered."

"Yeah, you lose ten, twenty grand, no big deal. How did you get all this money? Rich parents?" she asked, persistent.

He was tiring of her questions.

"Let's just say I left home with some cash."

"Must be nice."

Jake was pondering how much to reveal of his life.

"I came here for a reason. I needed to get away and wanted to live my life the way I chose."

"I know what you mean."

"Why did you move here?"

"Same reason, had to get away. Circumstances changed, and it was time for me to start over. It's really none of my business what you do, I got carried away expressing my opinion. I didn't mean to intrude."

"I like to talk about what I enjoy most, even if I'm speaking to a skeptic."

"My shift is over, and I'm going down the street to the bookstore, for a book fair. Would you like to come along?"

"A book fair. I haven't heard that terminology since middle school."

"I know it probably sounds boring, but I love books, and my favorite author will be there. There'll be others, too. You should come, it will be fun."

He saw her eagerness and couldn't help but oblige.

"It might be interesting."

"Great, I'll be back in a minute."

She got up from the table and went to the employee lounge. Summer removed her apron, applied a lip gloss, and grabbed her purse returning to see Jake waiting at the door.

"It's only a couple blocks away."

They walked along the sidewalk.

"How long have you been here?" she inquired.

"Two months, how about you?"

"Three years. My parents were killed in a car accident during my first year in college. I have an older sister, but she was already married and lived in another state. She'd just had a baby when it happened. I didn't want to stay in my hometown because everything reminded me of the life I no longer had. We sold our parent's house and with my share, I took to the road and this is where I stopped."

"That must have been hard."

"It was, but I needed to leave and start over."

"What about you?"

"I have an older brother."

The subject was dropped when they arrived at the Quail Ridge Bookstore.

"Here we are," she said, standing outside the entrance.

"Let's go meet your favorite author," Jake said, glad the subject had changed.

They meandered around the tables with books lined in a row. Jake followed Summer as she perused the covers picking up a book, and then setting it back on the table.

"It's good to get out and do something different," she told him.

"This is certainly different."

"I just have enough for one."

"That won't do, I've got this."

"No, I didn't mean for you to buy the books," she said, realizing how that must have sounded.

"I want to, and besides, you are going to owe me a month of Romano's, you remember that."

"I haven't forgotten."

"So many books and they are all good," she said.

"I thought you came to see your favorite author."

"I did and that's the book I will buy, but I wanted to browse through these first."

She walked over to the table of a woman autographing books, and requested a copy.

"Who do I make this out to?"

Jake spoke up.

"Make this to Summertime."

Summer turned and looked at him.

"That's really bad."

"I know, but didn't you say you were born in the summer?"

"I did."

Summer focused on the author.

"I've read all your books."

"Thank you, I hope you've enjoyed them."

"I have, and can't wait to read this one."

The author smiled at the couple and handed the book to Summer.

"Enjoy."

"I will."

"Let's go to the next table," Jake said.

"I can only afford one book, and I have it."

"I said, I was buying."

"You don't need to do that."

"I want to, let's go."

They walked to the next table.

"Make this to Summer Squash."

"No," she said, laughing.

Jake spoke first at the following author's table.

"Make it out to Summer Lovin'".

"That's funny," she said, giggling.

"Yes, it is," Jake agreed, grinning at her.

Summer was thrilled having three autographed books as they continued looking through the store. Since he was buying these for her, she decided to buy one for him, making her selection and handing it to him.

"What's this? The Sicilian Nobleman's Daughter," he read aloud, when she handed the book to him.

"It's a good book."

"I'll add it to the collection."

"No, this one I'm buying for you. My way of saying thank you to my noble man."

"You think I'm a noble man."

"You appear to be."

"That's cute, are you ready to go?" he asked.

"Yes, and you don't have to buy all these books for me, it's too much."

"I told you I was buying, and besides, can't return them now, they have your name on them."

"True."

They walked towards the front of the store, and Summer recognized a friend."

"Hi, Mr. Foster."

"Hello, Summer. Did you come for the book fair?"

He is a short elder gentlemen with thinning white hair and slight built. Obvious years outdoors reflected in his weathered skin.

The friend looked at the stack of books Jake was holding.

"I see you took advantage, couldn't get enough of the good word."

"I suppose not," Jake replied, puzzled.

Jake didn't realize he was in a Christian bookstore, not paying attention to the titles.

"Mr. Foster, I'd like you to meet a new friend, Jake Abraham. Jake, this is Joseph Foster."

They shook hands.

"Very nice to meet you, Jake."

"You too."

"Jake is new to the city," Summer told him.

"Welcome, it's wonderful to have a newcomer. How did you two meet, if you don't mind my asking?"

"He came into the coffee shop."

"Best coffee in town, and a good place to make a friend."

"It appears to be," Jake replied, looking at Summer.

"Do you have a church home yet?" Mr. Foster asked.

"No, no I don't. I've only been here a couple of months," Jake replied, surprised by the question.

"Well, you must join us at the New Life Fellowship Church down the road on the left. We welcome young people like yourself. Young members in the church keep us old ones on our toes," he said with humor.

"You should come, Jake," Summer said, encouraging him.

"It's perfect for people who just want to dive right in. I hope to see you there, you'll be most welcomed," Mr. Foster commented.

Jake glanced at Summer, but didn't answer. Mr. Foster redirected his attention to her.

"See you on Sunday. Jake, it was great to meet you. Hope to see you again, maybe in church.

I'll leave you young people to get on with your business. I came to check out some of the new authors."

"Enjoy yourself," she said.

"I intend too."

"Can we leave now?" Jake asked, feeling uncomfortable.

"Sure."

They stood in line at the register and ten minutes later were on their way back to Siesta. Summer spoke first.

"You know, Mr. Foster had a great idea. Will you come to church with me?"

"I'm not the church going type."

"I didn't realize there was a type. What do you mean, exactly?"

"I'm not comfortable in that environment."

"What environment? You mean among Christians."

"I guess that's what I mean."

Summer thought about what Jake said.

"Are you uncomfortable with me?"

"No, not unless you're going to start preaching."

"If I were to talk about God, would that bother you?"

"I gave up on God a long time ago."

"Why?"

Jake didn't want to get into a discussion about his faith but offered a short explanation.

"When my brother and I were young, we went to church as a family. Our Mom insisted, but I haven't been in years, actually since her death."

"I'm sorry to hear about your mother."

"Thanks."

"Maybe it's time to return."

"I don't think so."

"It can be a way of starting over. It's what saved me after my parents died. I got the job at the coffee shop and met Mr. Foster. I don't know what I would have done without him and the church, they became my family. You should come with me and try it," Summer said, gently encouraging him.

"I'll think about it."

"I hope you do," she said, not giving up.

They stopped outside the cafe's entrance.

"Thanks for accompanying me to the bookstore, and for the books. Will I see you again soon?"

"I'll be by for coffee."

"Okay."

Jake handed her the books keeping the one she bought for him.

"See you later," he said, leaving her standing there.

He was ready to check his investment. Jake felt he had been sucked into Summer's world and found it unsettling. A little too much goodness for his taste.

Summer watched him walk away wondering what she might have said that caused him to rush off once they arrived at Siesta. She sighed and went inside feeling a need to apologize again the next time she saw him.

Chapter 16

William was worried about the business, and spent the entire day going over the accounts. They had dealt with worse times in past years, but it bothered him that perhaps they wouldn't overcome as easily, lack of rainfall can be devastating. It wasn't realistic to rotate the water tanks with the extended sprinkler arms because they only had two and the task required several. It would be nearly impossible to water the entire acreage, and do so day after day. He didn't even know if the two wells on the property still had water.

Seth walked into his father's office and took a seat.

"I haven't seen you outside today."

"I needed to go over the books."

"What are you looking for?"

"I'm concerned we may run short this season," William told him.

"How short?"

"That's what I'm trying to figure out. I have some projected numbers. If we stay in a drought, we'll lose significant crop which means revenue will be drastically reduced."

"I can see about getting more water tanks."

"It would take more water than we can pump, if the wells aren't dried up, and have to be done continuously until it rained. I don't see that as solving the problem."

"We have to do something," Seth told him.

"I know that. What I don't know is what to do."

"Do we have any outstanding invoices? Maybe we should have Mrs. Grey give the vendors a call and lean on them to pay. Would that help?"

"She has already checked the accounts. They are set up on thirty day credit, and all the vendors have been real good about paying, I'm thankful for that."

Seth was silent for a moment, thinking.

"There is another way."

"What would that be?" William asked, looking at his son.

"Use my inheritance."

"No."

"Yes, you gave Jake a million bucks, so I assume I must have the same amount sitting in a portfolio, so use it."

"No, Seth. As with Jake, that's all I have for you. I won't take your money and put it into the farm."

"I'm telling you, it's okay."

"It isn't okay with me. If we spend that money, I will have nothing to give you. It wouldn't be fair to you, Seth. I can't do that."

Seth watched his father closely and appreciated that he wanted to be fair, but now wasn't the time to be concerned about that.

"We use the money, or we could lose everything," Seth said, pressing his point.

"I would rather lose the farm than leave you with nothing in the end."

"This farm is my life, Dad. You let me drive that tractor when my feet could barely touch the pedals. I grew up here, and I'm going to die here just like grandpa and great-grandpa. I will gladly give everything I have to keep this farm. Besides, what am I going to do with that kind of money, I'll never leave this farm to spend it."

He knew Seth meant every word, but it bothered William to take from his son to keep the business going.

"I'll think about it. In the meantime, let's pray for rain, that would solve part of the problem."

Seth noticed Mrs. Grey wasn't at her desk and glanced at his wristwatch, it was almost six o'clock. He went out the front door towards the barn, but stopped midway and looked at the fields. He would do whatever it took and wasn't concerned about the money. All he ever cared about was the farm, and now it was in jeopardy. He had no intention of losing the only thing that mattered to him.

Seth entered the barn, turned an empty pail upside down, and sat on it to think of things that might help the economics of the business, but nothing came to mind. There were no areas to cut because they handled it very frugally. Seth decided if he couldn't persuade his father to use his inheritance, maybe Mr. Farris could convince him.

William left the office and went to the kitchen, took out two frozen meals and placed them one at a time in the microwave. While they heated, he leaned against the kitchen counter in despair. He thought about Seth's offer but couldn't bring himself to take from his son, even though he understood how Seth felt because he felt the same way. He grew up on this land just as he had raised his sons, and it would leave a deep void if he had to let it go, not even sure he could do it.

His mind drifted to Jacob and wondered what his youngest might be doing at this very moment, and could only hope and pray he was well and living his life the way he desired. Saddened by everything, he thought of Marybeth as he often did, still missing her. She was the one constant in the family, the glue that held them in place. He took a plate of spaghetti and meatballs to the table but instead of eating, rested his head in his hands, and that was how Seth found him.

"Are you alright?"

"I'm fine, your dinner is on the counter."

Seth glanced over and back at his father.

"Thanks."

He washed his hands at the sink, took the plate and joined him.

"Dorothy is a good cook," Seth said.

"Yes, she is. Been faithful all these years since Marybeth," William said, agreeing.

"No one can replace mom, but we needed someone to cook and clean. I think we would've starved if not for her," Seth told him.

William knew Seth was attempting to make conversation other than discussing the farm, but he wasn't interested.

"I wonder what Jake is doing?" William asked.

"I don't really care."

"I do, and you should too."

William glanced at Seth without saying another word. The remainder of the meal was in silence. Afterwards, William went into the living room to read his Bible, something he did more consistently since Jake left. He asked God to keep a watchful eye on his youngest, to provide rain and protect the farm.

Chapter 17

Frank and Laura were attending the forty-fifth wedding anniversary of one of Frank's closest friends, Robert and Sally Winford. Laura was getting dressed in the bedroom while Frank waited in the kitchen.

"Come on, Babe, let's get this thing over with."

Frank didn't care for social events. He spent enough time dealing with customers at his restaurant, so when not there, he liked his privacy at home.

"Frank, it's fashionable to be late to parties, and I think people expect it."

"Well, for you maybe, but I'm tired of going to these things. I'd like to stay home one night. Seems we are always having some social event to waste my time."

"These are your friends and business associates."

"It doesn't change how I feel about parties."

"You have to make an appearance. We don't have to stay long, and besides their anniversary parties are always fun. You know you can't miss this, Bob and Sally would be disappointed."

He changed the subject noticing the small vase of flowers on the counter.

"Who bought you flowers?"

"They came this afternoon from Jake."

Laura walked into the kitchen, and turned asking Frank to zip her low-cut black evening dress. Frank obliged and leaned forward kissing her bare shoulder.

"Why is he buying you flowers?"

"He wanted to thank me for recommending the condo."

"How nice of him. A little skimpy, don't you think?"

"You never complained before," Laura responded, looking down at her dress.

"Not you, the flowers. Big investor, and he gives you sprigs. Looks like he got them at K-Mart."

She ignored his comment.

"He seems good at what he does, and could be useful for both of us. You'd love the car he drives."

"I'll bite, what does he drive?"

"A Maserati."

"I'm so impressed," he replied, mocking.

"You should be."

"Maybe we should stay home tonight and have our own party," he told her.

"We can have our party later, but right now we have to think of what is in your best interest. Staying in touch with your associates is important," she said, walking towards the door.

"Always thinking of an angle."

"Of course, and you expect it of me."

"That I do."

As they drove across town, Laura brought the subject of Jake up, again.

"I'll be spending time with Jake. He's asked me to show him around the city, and it'll give me an opportunity to learn more about him."

"Is that necessary?"

"He's got money. I don't know how he got it, but he drops hundred dollar bills everywhere he goes, and he wears expensive clothes, a fancy watch, and don't forget that car. I know from Sandra, he paid cash for the condo. He's a walking bank, and it would behoove us to see if he could be helpful in your arena," she explained.

"He's very young to have that kind of money," Frank admitted.

"Exactly, either his daddy's rich, or he's an astute investor. When I first met him, he said he followed the stock market. He might make you a wealthier man, Frank."

Frank glanced in her direction.

"Do you think I need more money?"

"It never hurts to have more."

"Fine, go sniff around and see what you can find out."

Frank pulled off the street into a gated community and stopped by the guard.

"The Winford party."

"Invitation, sir," the guard requested.

Frank looked over at Laura as she pulled out a small card from her purse and handed it to him.

"Here you go," Frank said, giving it to the guard.

"Take the first left, the third house on the right."

"I know where it is, thanks."

The gate was lifted, and Frank slowly drove through the neighborhood passing other vehicles on curbside and parked in front of the house. It was a large two-story ranch-style home with grey brick exterior. The party was in full swing when they entered a massive room with a high wood-beamed ceiling and mocha colored walls. The furniture was dark walnut with black and beige fabric sofas and matching chairs. Classical music permeated the room.

They quickly mingled with the guests recognizing many who were regulars at Frank's restaurant. Laura loved to attend parties, refining her acting skills and excused herself to pursue her agenda in looking for the next golden opportunity. It was the best way to meet prospective business men with money they were willing to spend.

"I'll catch up with you later," she told Frank.

He leaned in and whispered in her ear.

"Go do your thing."

She smiled at him before leaving his side. Crowds were her favorite as she watched the guests and listened to conversations. She monitored how they dressed, and most importantly, what they were discussing. After an hour, Laura met up with Frank.

"Gentlemen, if you will excuse us, I'm taking Laura home," he told the men in the group.

Taking Laura's arm, he led her away.

"We need to find Bob and Sally," he said.

Frank searched the big house and found his friend entertaining in another room. Frank extended his hand to Bob, a husky man in his late sixties.

"Congratulations on another year of married bliss."

"Thanks, Frank. Glad you could make it," Bob replied.

"I haven't seen Sally," Frank mentioned.

"She's around here somewhere, probably in the kitchen with her women friends."

"I'll find her before we leave."

"I see the restaurant business is doing good."

"You won't hear me complain."

"I'll give you a call next week. I have a business proposition for you," Bob told him.

"You know I like to hear about those. I'm taking Laura home, so enjoy your party."

Just as predicted, Sally was in the kitchen, and Frank walked up and gave her a gentle hug.

"You are looking lovely this evening."

A striking woman with short black hair and deep blue eyes in her sixties graciously accepted his embrace.

"Frank, darling, so glad you came."

"You know I wouldn't miss this special occasion."

She noticed Laura standing beside him.

"Laura, good to see you too."

"Congratulations."

"Thank you."

There had been enough parties throughout the years, that Sally was aware Frank and Laura were a couple.

"I just spoke with Bob, and he appears to be doing well."

"You know Bob, always dabbling into something to get that next thrill. I'm sure he's getting into trouble as we speak," she said, laughing.

"Did he tell you of his latest venture?"

"No, he didn't mention it."

"He will. Looking for ways to spend his retirement. He wants to buy a racing car team," Sally said.

"You mean a racing car."

"No, honey, I mean the entire team. You know the car, the mechanics, and all the stuff that goes with it," Sally told him, lightly touching Frank's arm.

"That's a sizable project."

"The bigger the better for Bob, that's what he likes."

"I wish him luck."

"You and me both," she said, chuckling.

Sally lived a luxurious lifestyle and never complained how her husband made his fortune. They had more money then they could spend, which was one of the reasons to not miss their parties. Frank and Laura said their farewells, and left as unobtrusively as they arrived.

Once they settled in the car, Laura spoke up.

"See, that wasn't so bad."

Frank glanced at her.

"Of course not."

"You know how important it is to make appearances. Never know who you might cross paths with. These are wealthy people, who have wealthier friends," she reminded him.

"We didn't walk away empty handed. Got a tidbit of news about the racing team. Might be something there for you," she continued.

"That's what I have you for, to remind me of these things."

The remainder of the drive to the condominium was in small talk. When they entered the apartment, Laura threw her coat on the sofa and turned her back to Frank.

"Unzip me."

Frank accommodated and then removed his jacket. While she went into the bedroom to change, he walked over to the small bar near the kitchen and poured a whiskey. Laura came back wearing a soft pink chenille robe. She took his drink and sat on the sofa. He poured another and joined her.

"Are you disappointed in the evening?" he asked.

"A little, you know I pride myself on what I do."

"And you are good at it."

"There's always another opportunity."

"Yes, and one I'm going to start on first thing in the morning."

Frank frowned.

"Jake," she said.

"Back to Jake, the supposedly rich young man. Remember, operative word is supposed. Tread with caution, love. He may not be what you think."

"That's what I intend to find out, shouldn't be hard to do."

"Enough talk about business, now it's time for our party."

Frank took the drink from her hand and placed it alongside his on the sofa table. He leaned in and kissed her passionately, then draws away nipping at her neck and shoulders.

"Babe, let's finish this in bed," he whispered.

He stood up and reached for her hand leading her to the bedroom.

Chapter 18

Jake returned to Siesta a few days after attending the bookstore with Summer. He immediately noticed Mr. Foster standing at the far end of the counter, and not in the mood to be bombarded by Summer or her friend, he quickly decided to place his order to go. Summer was preparing a coffee when she saw Jake standing at the counter.

"Want your usual?"

"Hello Jake, good to see you again," Mr. Foster said.

Jake turned and nodded, but focused on Summer.

"Yes, but make it to go."

"Not sticking around to study your stocks today?"

"Nope, got somewhere to be."

"Going to a world conquering seminar?" she said, sarcastically.

"You guessed it."

Jake left the counter to sit at a chair near the front window and wait. Summer gave Mr. Foster the coffee she prepared.

"What's wrong with your friend today?" he asked, glancing at Jake.

"I don't know, but I think he's avoiding me."

"I'm sure he'll come around when he's ready."

Summer glanced in his direction.

"I need to go make his drink, talk to you later."

Mr. Foster took his coffee and sat down at his usual table. He didn't think it was his business to interfere with Summer and her young man. Summer made the coffee and snapped a lid on it as Jake handed her a five dollar bill.

"Keep the change."

He picked up the hot cup and turned to leave.

"Jake."

"What?"

"Did I say something to offend you?" she asked, straightforward.

"No, I'm just in a hurry today."

"Are you sure?"

"Got a lot on my mind, and I have to go. I'll catch you later."

Summer was positive she said something, and wondered if it had to do with their conversation about church. Business was light, so she sat with Mr. Foster.

"I see your friend left."

"He didn't want to talk, I wonder if I've said something."

"Whatever is bothering him, he has to deal with it."

"It might have to do with our conversation about attending church. When we left the bookstore, I asked him to come to church with me, but he wasn't interested."

"Perhaps, he's not."

"He used to go to church when he was a kid, but stopped after his mother died."

"Well, it's our job as Christians to bring him back into fellowship. You'll find out in due time what has him upset."

"I need to get back to work, thanks for the chat."

"I'm always here for you."

Summer returned to wiping down the countertops and brewed a fresh pot of coffee. She contemplated what to say to Jake the next time she saw him, hoping it would be soon.

Jake had invested a serious amount of money and was anxiously waiting to see the outcome. If it went in his favor, he would make a hefty salary for one days work. Not in the mood to hang around the coffee shop and get into a debate about his lifestyle, or worse a lecture on the sins of a wayward soul, Jake walked along the sidewalk and sipped his coffee.

Summer seemed to be in his face each time he went to Siesta, and was growing weary of her endless questions. He wasn't interested in a relationship besides Laura, and expected Summer's intentions were more than a friendship. He thought she was a sweet girl with a compassionate heart, but her forwardness wasn't what he wanted right now. He was drawn to Laura's maturity and free-spirited nature. There was a haughtiness that he found attractive, and if this investment paid off, he considered asking her to celebrate with him.

Chapter 19

Jake had a good feeling and went to a nearby grocery store to buy a bottle of champagne, believing he would be celebrating soon. Spending the remainder of the afternoon flipping through cable stations on the television with nothing catching his attention, he grabbed the laptop sitting on the coffee table, hoping there would be some news on the trade. His face light up, and a big smile crossed his lips.

"Yes," he said aloud, pumping his fist in the air.

"Oh my gosh, I did it. I really did it."

He tossed the laptop on the sofa and jumped up dancing in a circle. Elated with his return on the investment, Jake couldn't wait to share his news and took the bottle of champagne, and knocked on Laura's door. When she opened, he held up the bottle.

"Any interest in sharing this with me?" he asked, with a grin on his face.

"Are you celebrating?"

"I am. Let's just say that I made a killing today."

"Really, how much of a killing?"

"Enough that I could have sailed over here in my new yacht, if I wanted to."

"Wow, that much. I'm impressed."

She looked at the bottle.

"News this special, and you're celebrating with bad champagne."

"Bad champagne," he repeated.

"Yes, really bad."

"The guy at the store said this was the best, not so?"

"No. Why don't we go to Frank's and get the good stuff, and we can celebrate there. I have an idea how we can better spend your money."

"You think so."

"Yes, I can show you how to party," she told him, teasingly.

Jake wasn't interested in going to Frank's restaurant, hoping for a private celebration.

"I thought maybe just you and me," he told her.

"That sounds wonderful, but there's someone I want you to meet, and he'll be at the restaurant this evening, you might want to talk business."

"Are you my new broker?" Jake asked, harshly.

"I can be, you need to meet him," she said, persistently.

It wasn't the way he wanted to spend the evening, but if it was the only way to have time with Laura, he would do it.

"Alright, let's go."

"Come on in, and give me a minute to change."

Jake entered the apartment, putting the bottle on the kitchen counter.

"Make yourself at home."

Jake studied several framed photographs on the end tables. He leaned forward for a closer look and recognized Frank in each one with a younger Laura. She returned to the room.

"All the pictures are of you and Frank."

"Yes, I told you we're friends. Shall we go?"

"Sure."

Jake drove them to the restaurant. Laura walked passed the hostess and continued to the lounge where a man was waiting at the bar. Jake saw this was preplanned.

"Hello, Evan."

A short slender man with curly brown hair turned.

"Laura, sweetie, good to see you."

"Evan, I have someone I want you to meet."

"This is Jacob Abraham. Jake, Evan Parker."

The men shook hands.

"Evan is a film producer as well as a great writer and director," she said, singing his praises.

"You don't say," Jake said, eyeing him closely.

"Yes, and he just finished writing an amazing script for a movie production."

"What is this amazing script about?" Jake asked, showing the expected interest.

Knowing Laura was an actress, he could understand her enthusiasm for a movie project.

"It's about the hollowness and angst of living in today's world. All the pressures that come with the chaos that's swirling all around us. It's about the inner luminosity that we have going dark and coming out. All the uncertainty we feel from change," Evan stated, passionately.

"That sounds deep," Jake told him.

"Oh yes, my friend, and it gets much deeper then that. The story reaches the very soul of man and strips him down to barbarism."

Jake doubted Evan's sanity, while Laura listened eagerly.

"It has a great role for a lead actress. I know it'll make a load of money, but we just need to get some investors to support the project. We need a lead investor," Laura told him.

"It's got box office hit written all over it. These are the kind of scripts that are trending all over the world," Evan said.

"I should be spending my money on a movie that you can star in," Jake said, bluntly.

Laura was surprised by his astuteness, something she wasn't expecting.

"It would be a good investment. We need just enough to break the ice," she said, recovering quickly.

"How much of an icepick are we talking about?"

Laura and Evan share a look, Evan answered.

"Initially, five hundred thousand would get us started, but in the end about two million."

"You are wanting me to invest half a million dollars into your movie project," Jake said, incredulously.

It literally shocked Jake that Laura would expect him to hand over such a sizable amount of cash for a movie production, so she could play the principal role.

"We need to find a lead investor to show other investors that someone believes in the project, and then other investors will see it as a solid investment and follow, it's not so much money," Laura said, pressing the point.

Before Jake could respond, Frank interjected his thoughts having eavesdropped on the conversation.

"From what I hear, it's about a day and a half of work for you," Frank mentioned.

"A good day and a half, maybe."

"You should do it," Frank told him.

"Why don't you do it, Frank?"

"Oh, I've had my time in show biz, I'm in the restaurant business now. You should help Laura, she's a great actress."

Jake looked at Laura.

"I'm surprised you wouldn't do this for Laura, being she's your friend," Jake said, countering.

"Let's just say I've done my share."

"If you aren't interested, then why should I be?"

"Do it for Laura," Frank insisted.

"I've got customers waiting, I'll let you two settle this."

Frank walked away. Evan is waiting with anticipation believing this is his opportunity to move forward with his production, while Laura sees the caution in Jake. She needs to apply pressure before Jake loses interest as he wasn't jumping into spontaneous agreement.

"The best thing about being the lead investor is that you have the opportunity to meet with other investors, people with money. The circle of people you want to be around who might get you involved in some of their other projects. You could be somebody important."

"That may be true, but it's still a hefty amount."

"Think about all the rewards," she replied with a smile.

"I need to think about this."

"Okay, but don't take too long. It's a great opportunity, and I want you to be the lead, so you will have complete control."

Laura wasn't expecting Jake to turn her down, but he wasn't the naive young man she figured him to be. Sometimes desperate times required desperate measures, and Laura realized this would be one of those occasions. Long ago, she made the decision to do whatever the circumstance required to get what she wanted. When Frank parted from the conversation, she had given him a special look.

Chapter 20

Jake and Laura occupied a corner at the bar and ordered drinks while she continued to persuade him to release his money. Evan left Laura to handle the situation.

"So, what do you think of the idea?" she asked.

"Oh, I can see how this would be good for you."

"Also for you, we could be partners."

"How do you figure that?"

"You supply the money, and I the talent."

Laura played with her wine glass, slowly running her third finger around the rim as she studied Jake.

"I see."

"I know it's a considerable amount of money, but you can make this and more in a day."

"I like to be sure of my investments, especially if I'm investing outside the market. We don't even know if the movie will payback at the box office."

"So you don't believe I'm a good investment?"

"Don't know, I've never seen you act in anything."

"Are you doubting this will be a box office hit?"

"Nobody can predict the future, it's a huge risk."

"Is that what's holding you back?"

Jake was tiring of the conversation. He didn't appreciate being pressured and especially over money.

"Let me think about it," he said, wanting to end the discussion.

"Don't take too long, someone else might beat you to the lead."

Jake realized she would have the last word. He had too much to drink and was feeling the effects of mixing his liquor.

"Are you ready to leave?" he asked.

"I am."

They left the restaurant at midnight and Jake was grateful for not running into Frank again. The drive to the condominium was in small talk. After an evening of being hammered about the movie production, there wasn't much Jake felt like discussing, Laura was definitely on one track.

Taking the elevator, Jake pressed the buttons for the fourth and seventh floors. When the door opened to Laura's floor, she pushed the bottom to close it and began ascending. Jake looked at her puzzled.

"What are you doing?"

She smiled at him without answering. The elevator stopped, and she took hold of his arm and gently pulled him in the direction of his apartment. Standing outside his door, she leaned into him.

"Let's not end the night just yet," she told him, seductively.

He unlocked the door and they went inside. Before Jake could put his keys in his pocket, Laura grabbed him behind the neck with both hands and drew his face towards her planting her mouth on his. At first Jake is taken off-guard, but she held tight pressing her body against his, breaking down his reserve. She wrapped her arms around his waist and drew him even closer.

Jake couldn't resist her affections realizing from the moment he saw her sitting across from him in the restaurant, he wanted her. She was throwing herself at him, and he wasn't thinking of a reason to refuse. Suddenly, he becomes just as amorous with neither taking their hands off the other.

"Let's go to the bedroom," she managed to whisper, breathless.

Jake didn't answer, but swayed her in that direction kissing as they made their way to his bed. With only a few short hours of sleep in the early morning, Jake awakened to the sun shining through his sheer drapes, and shaded his eyes until they adjusted to the brightness. As he gained awareness, he recalled the night and rolled over expecting to see Laura asleep beside him, but the bed only had one occupant. He closed his eyes and laid there not knowing what to expect when he faced her again, and couldn't deny that he wanted this between them.

Jake sat at the edge of the bed and held his throbbing head. Once the pounding had subsided, he stood up making his way to the bathroom for a cold shower. Feeling only slightly better, he went into the kitchen and downed two aspirin with a glass of water, put on his sunglasses, and took off for the elevator. He needed a bolder blend of coffee then what he had in his kitchen. As the elevator passed the fourth floor, he thought of Laura and what was going through her mind. How did she feel about what happened between them? For a fleeting moment, he wondered if it was planned, but he didn't want to let his thoughts take him in that direction.

He went to Siesta after leaving the complex with the crisp morning air feeling good against his still throbbing head. The coffee shop was very busy, and Summer had just finished an order when she noticed Jake.

"Good morning. What's with the sunglasses?"

"Bright outside."

"What can I get you? The usual."

"No, make it a dark roast with two shots of expresso, black, no cream."

"Wow, that's a bit strong."

Jake took off his sunglasses, and she saw he wasn't looking good.

"Are you feeling okay?"

"Not particularly."

"What's wrong? You don't look well."

"Nothing, got things going on."

"And that makes your appearance a little off."

Jake shrugged off her remark and paid for the coffee. He left the counter and took a seat at a small table away from the bright light shining through the front windows. Summer postponed making his coffee and motioned for the other girl to take her place at the counter. She followed him to the table and sat down.

"You haven't been acting your normal self. Is there anything I can help you with?"

Jake looked at her puzzled.

"Nope."

"You don't seem as happy as when you first moved here, or is it me. Did I say something to offend you?"

"I'm happy."

"Really."

"Yes, really."

"Jake, I want to be here for you, I want to help."

"I'm fine, and there is nothing in my life that requires your help."

That stung, but Summer was persistent.

"I don't know what is going on, but obviously something is bothering you. These past couple of times I've seen you, you've been distracted and distant. If you aren't willing to share your problem with me, then I suggest you turn it over to God, and trust Him to take care of the matter for you."

He didn't need a sermon.

"You know what I think?" she continued.

"No, but you're going to tell me," he said, agitated.

She ignored his comment.

"I think this is going to be good for you. Staying away from your family, remove all the distractions, and maybe come face to face with yourself and find your purpose."

Jake was irritated with her forwardness.

"Are you my shrink, now? Look, you don't have to worry about me, it has nothing to do with you."

"So, there is something bothering you."

"Maybe, but it's for me to work out. You don't need to concern yourself with my life."

Summer didn't know him, and he owed her no explanation. His life was his business, and he wasn't going to listen to a lecture from someone he just met.

"Look, I appreciate your concern for me. It's sweet, really. If I've seemed distant with you, then I apologize. There are things going on right now that I need to take care of," he told her, trying to be polite and end the conversation.

Summer wasn't content, but accepted it.

"Okay."

She hesitated for a moment.

"My small Bible study group is getting together later today. Maybe you might like to come with me."

"I don't think so. I have things to do, but thanks for the invite."

"I thought it might be nice to spend some time together."

Jake sees the sincerity in her expression, but isn't impressed with her persistence. The last thing he needed was someone else applying pressure for him to do something.

"I'm trying to balance some things at the moment, but I will try to make some time for you."

Summer was surprised by his comment.

"You don't have to consider it a chore, never mind."

"It will happen."

"That's okay. I understand you aren't interested, don't concern yourself," she told him, disappointed and hurt by his remark.

Summer went to make his coffee, and set it on the table in front of him.

"Here you go, extra strength."

"Thanks."

He watched her leave and felt guilty for being so direct, after all, she was trying to be friends. I'll make it up to her later, he thought. Jake took his computer from the backpack and put it on the table. He hesitated before opening it focused on Summer talking with another customer at the counter. Observing her while she worked, he didn't want to lead her into thinking he was interested more than as a friend.

He thought of last night with Laura and wondered what it meant, a one night stand, or the beginning of a relationship. Was she interested in him, or just his money? That was the question that stayed in the forefront of his mind, and he wouldn't have an answer until he saw her again.

The caffeine from the expresso helped with the hangover, and Jake was finally able to begin his work day. Summer left him alone, and he was grateful to have no further interruptions. Approximately an hour later, as she passed his table to deliver two lattes, Jake practically jumped out of his chair.

"No way," he said aloud, laughing.

"What's going on?" Summer asked, turning around to look at him.

"Check this out."

She leaned forward looking at the screen.

"I'm not sure what I'm looking at, but I'm guessing I'll be owing you some free coffee."

"All month long, Baby."

"Then I expect my tips to be bigger, Baby," she said, relieved he was being friendlier.

"I'll consider that."

"Tell me what happened?"

Excitedly, Jake explained.

"I took the profit that I made yesterday, doubled it, and reinvested back into the same stock and just quad-tripled my earnings," he told her, almost unbelieving himself.

"That's fantastic."

"No, it's more than fantastic, it's unprecedented."

"I'm happy for you, Jake."

"Thanks."

Summer walked away seeing his attention wasn't on her. Jake punched a few keys, closed the laptop, and dropped it into his backpack. He took the empty ceramic cup to the counter and handed it to Summer.

"Congratulations."

"Thanks, I'll see you around."

"Yeah, sure, I'm always here."

She couldn't hide her disappointment.

Jake left the coffee shop in a hurry to get back to his apartment. He had some serious thinking to do before investing further in this particular company's stock. Maybe he should consider Laura's movie project after all. The money was flowing in and things were definitely looking good.

Chapter 21

William stood on the porch and looked down the long driveway thinking about the day Jake drove away, and still no word from him. He worried for his youngest, not knowing where he was. He respected his son's privacy and assumed if something went awry, the police would notify him. It wasn't a comforting thought, but a realistic one.

Seth approached his father from the barn.

"We're going to lose significant crop if we don't get rain soon."

Seth referred to the crops as though they were something special in his care. To a farmer dedicated to the land as the Abraham men were, the harvest would be much more than yielding a profit.

"I know."

"We've got another problem, the engine on the tractor is down," Seth said, flustered.

"I thought we had it repaired."

"We did, but parts were replaced by Benwood."

"We don't do business with Benwood. Why did they do the repair?" William asked.

Seth looked at his dad with a knowing expression.

"Take a guess."

William understood and sighed.

"Didn't somebody tell Jake we don't use them."

"I did, but he didn't listen, and Mrs. Grey confirmed Jake approved it. Just another thing we have to go behind and clean up. He's not even here, and we're still dealing with his bad judgments."

William ignored Seth's comment.

"Let's get it fixed, we can't do without it."

"Already on it. Tractors and More is willing to do the repair on credit since we've been excellent customers for years."

"Good. I'm going into town, I'll see you later," William said.

William went inside leaving Seth standing alone. Seth wondered what business his father had in town, for he seldom ventured off the property, but figured he'd find out later and walked to the barn.

William drove to his friend's house, and Sid answered the door surprised to see him.

"Abe, what brings you to my neighborhood?"

"I should've called first, but can you spare an hour to grab some lunch?"

"Of course," he said, stepping outside.

They walked to William's SUV.

"Where would you like to go?" William asked.

"Any place is fine."

"What about Debbie's Diner?"

"Sure, she makes an excellent corned-beef sandwich with homemade potato salad. The thought of it is making my mouth water," Sid said.

Sid knew there was something on Abe's mind for him to stop by, unexpectedly. William drove the ten miles to the small family-owned diner where he and Marybeth used to patronize all those years ago. It brought back a rush of memories as he parked in front. Inside the diner, William automatically went to the back corner booth with Sid following. Once they sat down, he realized it was the same booth he and Marybeth always sat at. Must be subconscious to gravitate to this table, he thought.

"Is this okay?" William asked.

"Anywhere is fine."

A waitress took their drink order after handing them menus. She returned with two iced teas, and noted their request for two corned-beef sandwiches and potato salad.

"You seldom come into town, and not often to my place," Sid said, noticing William's worried expression.

"Needed to get away from the farm for a few hours."

"Since when do you need an excuse to leave."

"Not an excuse, exactly. Maybe I wanted a break to clear my head."

"Something on your mind?"

William sipped his tea.

"Many things these days."

"How can I help you?" Sid asked.

"Honestly, I'm not sure."

"Have you heard from Jake?"

"No, nothing," William said with a deep sigh.

"He's fine, Abe. We have all prayed for his welfare, and I know the Father is looking out for your son."

William ran his right hand up and down the glass of tea, and looked at Sid.

"I believe that."

"Then don't worry about him. God wouldn't want you to take back the very thing you gave him to handle."

"I know."

"How are things at the farm?" Sid asked, deliberately changing the subject.

"That's another issue, this drought isn't good for business."

"I imagine not."

William hesitated before speaking again, turning the subject to what was on his mind.

"I don't know if I will ever see Jake again. I think about him everyday, and feel as though I've lost two family members, Marybeth and now Jake," he said, pausing to collect his thoughts.

"I didn't have any say in Marybeth's untimely death, but perhaps things could have been different if I had been more supportive of Jake and involved in his interests. Maybe he wouldn't have felt the need to leave home to find in someone, or something else what I didn't give him," William said, unleashing his feelings.

Sid leaned back on the bench and listened attentively; however, hearing the emotional pain in William was disturbing.

"I can look back and remember the times he tried to share his ideas, and I shunned him, not deliberately, but by not encouraging him, I was rejecting him. I can't blame him for not wanting to be around any longer. I failed him."

Sid waited before speaking.

"I don't believe for a minute that you failed your son. I can't speak from personal experience since I wasn't blessed with children, but I've watched you through these years with your boys. You've poured out your love on them."

"It wasn't enough."

"Perhaps what Jake needed was something you couldn't give him. Have you thought of that?"

"No, I wasn't any good to Seth or Jake when Marybeth died. He went to college, and when he returned with ideas of making the farm better with new technology, I didn't take him seriously. That was his biggest complaint before he left."

"I'm sure he understood you weren't ready to make monumental changes in the business."

"I should've been a better father to both my sons. If I was, Jake would be home right now."

"I've seen the father you are, and can say without any doubt that you have done a great job raising your boys. Being a parent isn't an easy task. Are mistakes made along the way, definitely, but you can't take on the responsibility that Jake wanted to explore the world, and see what it has to offer. The chick eventually wants to leave the nest."

"Just because others in the family have had no desire to go exploring, doesn't mean Jake shouldn't be given the opportunity if he wants to take it," Sid continued.

The food arrived and the subject was changed. They chatted on other topics, and when it was time to pay, William picked up the check and drove Sid home.

"Abe, my advise is to stop blaming yourself, and stop worrying. Jake is doing what he wants to do, and besides, he will return home when he's ready, you can count on that."

"I just hope I'm still around when he does."

"You will be. Thanks for lunch, hope I was of some help."

"Appreciate the conversation," William told him.

Sid nodded.

He waved before walking into his house. William backed out of the driveway and headed towards the farm. He thought about their conversation and it made sense, but it still didn't relieve the blame he felt. There was nothing he could do but wait for his son to come home, and pray that he did.

Chapter 22

Jake walked into the complex debating whether to stop by Laura's apartment. He wanted to tell her the good news, and yet, was unsure how receptive she would be to seeing him. However, his exuberance overpowered his sensibility, and he went to her apartment and listened outside the door when he overheard voices. He pressed his ear closer to the door trying to determine the conversation, and who was with Laura and surmised it was Frank.

"You came home late last night."

"Are you keeping tabs on me?"

"Do I need to?"

"I thought we agreed to have an open arrangement," she said, reminding him.

"We do."

She changed the subject.

"You might want to know that Jake is loaded and making more money as we speak."

"And you know this, how?"

"I have my ways."

"No doubt you do."

"Do you think he will invest in your movie?"

"Not sure, but I'm working on it."

Jake couldn't make out the conversation, the voices were muffled but thought he may have heard his name. He went to his apartment, disappointed. He didn't like the fact that Frank was with her.

Frank and Laura continued their conversation.

"How much money do you think you can funnel out of him?" Frank asked.

"As much as he's got."

"Well, make sure he never finds out the truth."

"He won't find out."

"Just make sure he doesn't."

"Have I ever let you down, Frank?"

"No."

He took her chin and drew her face close and kissed her.

"How soon will we have the money?" he asked.

"Soon, I'm going up to visit him in a few minutes."

Frank smiled at her.

"You do that, I'm off. Are you coming by the restaurant later?"

"Planning on it, and hoping I'll have Jake with me to make that deal."

"That would be worth celebrating."

He pulled her into an embrace and kissed her before leaving. Laura walked into the bedroom to change her cloths, and touched up her makeup in the bathroom. After tucking the keys in her pocket, she took the elevator to Jake's apartment.

Jake was on the laptop when he heard the knock. Through the peephole, he saw Laura and opened the door.

"Hello," she said.

"Hi, yourself."

"May I come in?"

"Absolutely."

"I was hoping you would come down to see me this morning."

"I wasn't sure you wanted me to."

Jake didn't tell her he'd stopped by.

"Why wouldn't I want to see you, and especially after last night?" she asked with a mischievous smile.

Jake felt relieved.

"You mentioned spending some time together to see the sights of the city. Are you free today?"

"That'd be great. Give me a minute to shut down my computer."

"Are you working? I don't want to bother you if you're busy making money."

"It's fine, I can get back to it later."

"Let's go have some fun," she said.

Jake grabbed his jacket and slipped his arms into it. Laura stepped up to adjust the collar and stood close looking up at him.

"Kiss me."

Jake saw the sparkle in her beautiful blue eyes. He placed his thumb on her chin with the support of his index finger and lifted her lips to his. His kiss is unassuming as he gently applied pressure. When their lips parted, she smiled at him and put her hands on his face, drawing him to her and kissed him again.

"Maybe we should stay in today," she suggested.

"Now, why didn't I think of that?"

She kissed him repeatedly, stroking the fire that ignited in both of them until neither could get enough of the other. She tugged at his coat lifting it off his shoulders. Hours later, they discovered they were famished as Laura leaves his bed.

"I'm going to my apartment to freshen up. Come pick me up in thirty minutes, and we'll go have dinner."

Jake watched her dress but made no effort to get up. Before leaving the bedroom, she walked over to his side of the bed, and bent down to kiss him.

"Don't be late."

Jake laid there for a moment amazed at his good luck, for everything was going his way. He's got the money and the girl, and life couldn't be any better, he thought.

He threw the covers back, and got out of bed to shower. Twenty minutes later he was knocking on Laura's door.

She was waiting for him, and they left arm in arm.

"I'm starving, you wore me out," she told him, teasingly.

"I thought that was the other way around."

Riding down in the elevator, Jake spoke first.

"I take it we're going to Frank's."

"We don't have too, but he does have the best steak in town."

"I'm in the mood for a good steak," he said.

The hostess seated them, and a waitress immediately came to fill the water glasses and take their drink orders.

"Let's get a bottle of wine and celebrate," Laura said.

"Okay, what would you recommend?"

"Cindy, tell Joe to pick out the best," Laura told the waitress.

"Certainly."

A few minutes later, Frank walked up to their table carrying a bottle of wine already chilled in an ice bucket, with two long-stemmed glasses, and set it on the edge of the table.

"Hello Laura, Jake. May I do the honors?" Frank asked.

"Please," Laura said.

Having spent the day in bed with Laura, Jake was certain he had the upper hand over Frank. He was no longer intimidated by his presence; after all, Laura was with him.

"Enjoy your dinner," Frank told them.

"We will, Frank," Jake replied, arrogantly.

"That was nice of Frank, don't you think?"

"What, pouring our wine."

"No silly, giving us his blessings."

"Was that what he was doing? I thought he was pouring wine."

Laura laughed making Jake grin at her.

"So does this mean we're a couple?" he asked.

"I suppose we are."

"What about Frank?"

"I told you, Frank and I are good friends."

He looked at her while playing with the stem of his wine glass, and smiled. Cindy returned to the table to take their order.

"Prime rib, medium rare, baked potato, steamed broccoli," Laura spoke first.

"That sounds good, make it two."

"You got it, I'll be back to check on you."

"Thanks, Cindy," Laura said.

"Is it always this busy," Jake asked, looking around the room.

"Always, it's one of the best restaurants in the city."

"Must be."

"There's a party tomorrow night at Evan's house, a small gathering of friends. Would you go with me?"

"Why not, it might be fun."

"Great."

"Does this have anything to do with the movie project?"

"No, it's just a small party."

Cindy brought their dinner to the table, and they took their time eating, drinking, and chatting. Laura laughed easily which kept Jake in good spirits. He was enjoying himself, relaxed, and realized for the first time, he truly felt comfortable since arriving in the city. Finally, he had a place to belong.

Chapter 23

The next morning, Jake went to Siesta for his usual coffee, for it always tasted better then his home brew. He also wanted to apologize to Summer for the way he treated her during his last visit.

"You're back, I wasn't sure you'd return."

"Can I get a caramel latte?"

"Of course, anything else?" she asked, keeping the tone strictly business.

"Yes, a slice of the pound cake."

She rang up his order while Jake pulled out a twenty.

"No hundred dollar bill," she said, remembering the first day he came in.

Jake smiled while handing her the bill, and put the change in a large plastic bowl marked for tips and went to a table.

She brought the coffee and cake to him.

"At least you look better today," she told him.

"Listen, Summer, I want to apologize for the way I behaved. I wasn't myself the last time I was here, and I took it out on you."

"I agree with that."

She turned to walk away, but he called her back.

"I want us to be friends. I admit I might not always be the best, but since I come here for my coffee, I want us to be able to talk."

"No problem, I will give you a friendly smile just like I do all the customers."

"That's not what I'm talking about."

"I know what you're saying. I probably shouldn't have been so forward in my invitations. I've been thinking about our last conversation and realize I was too pushy, but I can plainly see you aren't interested. You know, the bookstore, the study group, talking about God, I get it. I do understand."

"You're right, God is not a focus in my life right now."

"He is in mine, and that would present a problem."

"It doesn't have to, if we don't let it."

"How do you figure that?"

"I'm not sure," he said, looking at her.

"That's what I mean. I've got to get back to work."

The conversation didn't go as Jake had expected. Now he felt worse then before, because he knew she liked him. Maybe she was lonely and reaching out for friendship, and he understood what that felt like.

He drank his coffee and ate the cake while watching her. There was something endearing about her nature. She smiled easily to all the people who came in, and some she chatted with. She glanced in his direction to see him raise his coffee cup, and Summer came over to his table.

"Yes, Jake, what can I get for you?"

"A cup of medium roast with cream."

"Sure."

She brought over a fresh cup and he handed her a five dollar bill.

"Keep the change."

"I'll put it in the tip jar."

He pulled out his laptop and sat for nearly two hours before looking at the wall clock to see it was nearly noon, and waved to motion Summer to this table.

"When do you get a lunch break?"

"Ten minutes. Why?"

"I want to take you to lunch."

"Why would you do that?"

"Will you have lunch with me?" he asked, ignoring her question.

She stared at him leery of the change in him, again.

"I suppose."

"Great."

Jake closed his laptop.

"I'll get my purse."

"How much time do you have?"

"An hour."

"Where do you normally go?"

"There's a deli two doors down. I usually eat there, it's close."

"Alright, let's go there."

They walked to the deli Summer frequented that served sandwiches, soups, and salads and waited in line to place an order. Jake paid while Summer located a table and sat down, and then joined her.

"Why did you want to have lunch?"

"Why not?"

"Because you've made it clear you aren't interested in doing things with me. Does this have anything to do with what I said earlier?"

"I felt you were pushing me in a direction I don't want to go," he told her, honestly.

"Are you referring to my being a Christian?"

"I don't mind you having your faith, I know what that's like."

"What happened to yours?" she asked.

He looked away for a moment before replying.

"It died with my mother."

"Will you tell me about it?"

Jake didn't want to go down memory lane and recall the emotions and heartache he was trying so hard to bury, but accepted he should give her an explanation.

"My mother was killed in a car accident when she was forty-nine."

"Was it a drunk driver?"

"No, just unfortunate timing. An icy road, and a truck out of control. One minute she was with us, and the next gone."

"Jake, that was devastating for you," Summer said, reaching across the table placing her right hand on his arm.

She understood what that felt like.

"When she was alive, we were your typical church-going family. Every Sunday morning, faithfully sitting in the front pew, but when she died, my father went into a deep depression, my brother took over the responsibilities of the family business, and I went to college. Nothing was ever the same."

Summer looked at Jake without saying a word. She could see the emotional injury he suffered, and didn't know how to help him. The silence was broken when their food was brought to the table.

"Jake, I'm so sorry."

"Yeah, me too. We better eat this food, you said your break is only an hour."

He wanted to change the subject. Summer felt compelled to help Jake overcome the heartache he carried deep within his soul, and knew God was the only way. She needed to think about this before speaking again on the subject. It made sense why he was so turned off to anything Christian.

The remainder of the lunch was small talk about his investments, stocks, brokers, and things that she knew interested him, and he livened up when speaking on this topic. They walked back to Siesta, and parted at the entrance.

"Thanks for the lunch, I enjoyed it," Summer told him.

"So did I, I'll see you around."

"You know where to find me."

Summer went inside and turned to see Jake still watching her, and waved before going to the employee lounge to drop off her purse and get her apron. She understood him better, and it made her feel good. Summer was on a mission to help him and knew Mr. Foster could give her wise counseling. She would speak with him the next time he came in.

Chapter 24

Jake attended Evan's party with Laura expecting an intimate gathering of a few friends as she had inferred; however, when they went inside the house, it was far from what he imagined.

"Laura, my sweet, I'm so glad you brought your friend," he said, meeting them at the door.

"Jake, good to see you, my man."

"Evan."

"Come on in and make yourselves at home, Laura will show you around. She comes to all my parties. Go meet my friends, and I'll catch up with you later," Evan said with a bright smile for Laura.

Standing in the middle of the living room, he took a survey of the guests, and a quick headcount showed about thirty people who had obviously been there for a while. The party was going strong with loud music, drinking, and dancing with some of the couples getting too affectionate. He looked at Laura in puzzlement.

"This isn't exactly the party atmosphere I expected."

"I told you it was some close friends."

"Friends getting very close," he countered.

"Is this the kind of parties you attend?"

"Yes, some of the people here are my friends, or we have worked together in the past."

Jake was more then surprised to learn this of Laura. He understood her to be a social person who enjoyed a good time, but this was beyond what he had considered. It was a very uninhibited group of people.

"Don't look so shocked. Come on, let's get something to drink, and I'll introduce you," she said.

Laura took his hand and led him across the room towards the kitchen where a bar was set up. They walked in to find a couple against a wall engaged in heavy kissing. Jake looked away, feeling he was intruding as Laura caught his expression.

"Jake, loosen up, it's a party. You're supposed to relax and have fun."

"It's a party, alright."

The couple remained oblivious to anyone's presence, and Jake tried not to stare.

"People get a little loose at Evan's parties."

"I can see that."

He looked back at Laura.

"Why are we here?"

"To have fun, and besides, there are some people I want you to meet."

"People in the entertainment business."

"Exactly."

"Still thinking of ways to spend my money," he said a bit too direct.

"I suppose you could see it that way. I prefer to think of it as helping to connect you with the right people that have money, so you could learn of their ventures and make more, but if you don't want my help, I'll leave you to your own devices."

"Let's go meet your people," he told her, already disillusioned.

They made drinks before returning to the living room, and Laura spotted the person she most wanted to connect with Jake. He wasn't taking the bait with Evan, so she thought of another means to the same end.

"Follow me," she said, taking off across the room.

Jake walked closely behind her with drink in hand as she approached a man in his late forties showing signs of gray threading through in his black hair.

"Hello, Laura. We seem to always meet at one of Evan's parties," he said.

"Peter, I'd like you to meet a friend of mine. This is Jacob Abraham, Peter Usherton," she said, making the introductions.

The men shook hands.

"Call me Jake."

"Jake, are you in the entertainment business?" Peter asked.

"No."

"Jake is new to our city, he's an investor," Laura said, making sure she pointed out his profession.

"What kind of investor?"

Jake paused before answering,

"I study the stock market, mutual funds, pending or recent patents, things like that."

"Impressive study for someone so young, a novice."

"I've been doing this for several years now."

"You don't say."

"Yeah, I do," Jake said, agitated.

He intended to be taken seriously regardless of his age.

"Laura, where did you find this young man?" Peter asked, impressed.

"Oh, he found me," she replied with a smile.

Laura took hold of Jake's arm entwining hers in his.

"What do you do, Peter?" Jake asked, returning the question.

"I dab in a few things," he replied, deliberately being vague.

"Such as?"

"The entertainment business is one. I'm like the means behind the machine. What I mean by that is, I like to be in charge and orchestrate people and events to make things happen. Let me give you an example. Evan is in need of cash to turn a script he wrote into a movie. I personally have read the script, and it's plausible for a production. Laura is an actress wanting her big break. In fact, most of the people in this room are want-to-be actors who haven't made the scene," he said, laughing at his own pun.

Pausing, Peter looked around the room. Laura and Jake waited for him to continue.

"I consider my job as connecting the dots, the conductor at the orchestra."

"Do you put up your own money?" Jake asked.

"Now that's the beauty of it, I don't. I get investors, like yourself, to put up the real stuff. I simply control the outflow."

Jake pondered over his words.

"I see, like a director, or CEO of a conglomerate."

"Exactly, you catch on quick. I like him, Laura," Peter said, eyeing her.

"Maybe we can talk business," he continued, taking a card from his jacket pocket and handing it to Jake.

"Call me, could be some potentials."

Jake looked at the card.

"Maybe."

Laura understood the conversation was over.

"Come on, Jake, let's go dance."

Laura turned back and smiled at Peter, and he winked at her.

She and Jake walked to a somewhat secluded area, and Laura wrapped her arms around his neck as they swayed to the music coming from the stereo. She rested her head on his shoulder, pressing her body against his. Jake held her close intoxicated by the sweet fragrance of her hair and turned his nose into the soft blonde curls and inhaled. They didn't speak, simply enjoyed the embrace. When the music had stopped, she stepped back and looked deeply into his eyes. Jake was completely mesmerized by her, caught like a fly in a spider's web. Laura leaned in and gently kissed him.

The remainder of the evening was spent drinking, meeting people, and having identical conversations with a few dances in between. Jake was exhausted of hearing about movie projects, scripts that never left the shelf, unemployed actors waiting for their big break, and everyone wanting his money.

It was three in the morning when they arrived back at their apartment complex, and both were more than tipsy from the consumption of liquor. In the elevator, Laura spoke up.

"Jake, just drop me off at my place. I'll be sleeping off a hangover in the morning."

Laura fumbled to find the key in her purse, unlocked the door, and turned to kiss him.

"Go sleep it off, I'll see you tomorrow," she told him.

"Goodnight," he replied.

Laura walked inside and shut the door. Jake rode the elevator to the seventh floor, entered his apartment and went to the bedroom stripping clothes off. When he reached the bed, he was half undressed falling forward across the middle and passed out.

Chapter 25

Summer was pleased to see Mr. Foster enter the coffee shop. He took his place in line, and when he approached the counter, Summer spoke what was on her mind.

"Good morning, are you having your usual?"

"Yes, old habits are hard to break."

"I need to talk with you. Will you still be here in fifteen minutes?"

"Of course, anything wrong?"

"I'm not sure, I'll come over to your table later," she told him, seeing the line of customers standing behind him.

"You'll find me in my usual spot," he said, glancing to make sure his table was unoccupied.

About twenty-five minutes later, Summer joined him.

"Can I get you a fresh cup of coffee?" she asked, before sitting down.

"I could use another."

She made a fresh cup, and took it to the table.

"Here you go."

"Thank you, dear."

He took a sip.

"I still say this is the best coffee in town. Now, tell me what's happening."

"It's Jake."

"Of course, your young man."

"Technically, he's not my man, but he's lost and needs our help."

"Do you mean strayed from God."

"Exactly."

"I see. Let's pray for him," he said.

He reached across the small table for her hands and holding tight, they bow their heads.

"Dear heavenly Father, one of your sheep has wandered from the flock and needs to be shown the way back. Enlighten us to what we may do to help this young man. Use Summer as your vessel to bring him home to you. On the holy name of your son, Jesus, we pray, Amen."

"Amen."

"Now you have a big responsibility ahead of you," he informed her.

"I try to talk to him, but what I say pushes him further away."

"You'll know."

"I was hoping you could give me some advice."

"Have you seen him lately?"

"Yesterday he came in to apologize, and took me to lunch at the deli down the street."

"That's encouraging."

"It bothers him that I'm a Christian."

"Has he said something?"

"Yes, and no. He didn't mind that I am, but doesn't want to discuss it. His family used to go to church when he was younger, but when his mother died in a car accident, the family fell apart, and I don't think he has been in a church since," she explained.

Mr. Foster listened, attentively.

"Tragedy can bring someone closer to God, or drive them away."

"I understand that. For me, when my parents died, I didn't have anyone. I was on my own. Coming here, meeting you and joining the church saved me, and I have a new family. I want to show Jake that it is possible to start a new life, but the first step is to return to God."

"Your own experience has made you strong and wise. Perhaps, because the two of you have a similar tragedy with the loss of parents, you will be able to connect with him on that level."

Summer thought about it for a moment, and maybe there was a personal way to reach him.

"I wish I could get him to come to church with me. I invited him to my Bible study group, and he was practically appalled by the idea."

"You'll have to spend time with him, and create a comfort in your relationship whereby he becomes more favorable to the idea."

"That's hard to do because he only comes in a few times a week, and then sits glued to his laptop."

"You did have lunch together, that's promising."

"True, but if I'm the one asking him to go out, and the things I want to do aren't what he's interested in, we have a problem."

"I see your point."

"Do you think if I spoke with him, he might attend some seminars, or church events that are specific for the men of the congregation?"

"No, he would think we are ganging up on him."

"Then we must continue to pray for him. I'll put his name on the prayer list."

"I appreciate that. I've got to get back to work, thanks for the conversation."

"I'm always here for you, Summer."

Summer reached across the table and touched his arm before leaving him to sit alone. Throughout the morning, she thought about what Mr. Foster had said, make it personal. They did have something in common. Could she use that to her benefit to help him, she wondered.

She took her lunch at the deli, as usual. While eating a tuna salad sandwich with her head bent down reading a book, she didn't see Jake walk into the restaurant. He spotted her, placed an order, and went to sit down at her table. She looked up.

"Mind some company?"

"Jake, what are you doing here?" she asked, surprised to see him.

"It's a restaurant, and I came to eat."

She laughed at how ridiculous her statement must have sounded.

"Of course."

He noticed the large book she was balancing on her lap.

"What are you reading?"

"Physiology."

"That's heavy. Sounds like a college course I distinctly remember avoiding. The study of living organisms didn't go well with accounting and financial subjects."

"I don't suppose it would."

"Are you in college?"

"Yes, why? Did you think I was going to spend the rest of my life working in a coffee shop?"

"I never thought about it. I come in, see your pretty face, and get my cup of Java," he told her.

Summer smiled at him.

"So, what's your major?"

"Pathology."

"Like working in a lab and studying microscopic things in petri dishes?"

"Criminal Pathologist, to be exact."

"That's way out there. You mean examining crime scenes and gathering evidence to investigate"

"That's it."

"I'm impressed."

"Why?"

"I just didn't imagine you in such a serious career."

"What did you imagine? A secretary, or accountant, maybe an attorney."

"Something like that."

"No, I'm the more adventurous type, I like to unravel a mystery."

"When do you graduate?"

"Two more years. I started right out of high school, but when my parents died, I dropped out. I'll be one of those older graduates."

"Better to do it, then not at all."

"That's what I thought too."

His plate of food was brought to the table.

"When do you go to school?"

"At night. I work as many hours as I can at Siesta, and when I leave there, I go to the university library and study, then off to class."

"That makes for a long day."

"It does, but I'm used to it."

Jake took a bite of the sandwich thinking about their conversation, impressed with her ambition and realized how alone she was, and yet, making a life for herself. Not so different from himself, he thought.

Summer's lunch break was over, and Jake hurriedly finished.

"I need to get back," she told him, gathering her things.

He walked her to the coffee shop.

"See you later," she said, turning to go inside.

This time she didn't look back to see if he was still standing there, but walked directly to the lounge to put her things away. Jake stood on the sidewalk staring inside the glass door, and when he saw her come out with her apron on, he walked away.

Earlier, when he went inside the cafe and was told she was on a lunch break, he knew where to find her. For some reason, he felt the need to make amends.

Chapter 26

Frank knew Laura and Jake had attended Evan's party, something he refused to do. Allowing her time to recoup from the late night, he left her asleep and returned in the afternoon. They sat on the sofa, and she highlighted the evening.

"Do you think it's worth doing this?" Frank asked.

"I do. He made eighty grand in one day, and he's pulling money regularly. He knows how to make money."

"Really."

"Yes, faster than you're making it."

"You get him in, and we can change that. Do you think he'll contribute to the movie?" Frank asked.

"He's teetering on making a decision. I just need to push him a little more."

"How long is this going to take?"

"Maybe tonight, I'll bring him by the restaurant."

Jake decided to stop by Laura's apartment to see how she survived the party. He knocked on the door, and when she invited him in, he saw Frank sitting on the sofa. It bothered him to always find Frank in her apartment. Frank grabbed his jacket and left.

"Jake, nice to see you again. Babe, I'll see you later."

"Why is Frank always here?"

"We've already been over that. What brought you by?" she asked, deflecting any further questions.

"I wanted to see how you were doing after last night's party."

"Let's sit down."

Jake realized he was sitting in the same place Frank just vacated, and it reminded him of a turnstile.

"Have you given any thought to investing in Evan's movie?" she asked, getting straight to the point.

"Yes, it's been on my mind."

"What's the verdict?"

"I have a proposition for Frank."

"What does Frank have to do with you investing in the movie?"

"I need to talk to Frank first."

"Alright. What about this evening at the restaurant?"

"That'll be fine."

"Want to pick me up at six, and we'll go for dinner?"

"Sure."

"So what did you think of Evan's party?"

"It was something."

"Do you think there were any connections for future business opportunities?"

"Possibly."

"That's good."

Laura had the information she needed.

"I've got things to do before this evening," she said, wanting to end the conversation.

"No problem."

"See you at six," Laura told him.

"I'll be here."

Jake left her apartment puzzled and went upstairs to think this through. Why was Frank always with her? Even close friends didn't spend that much time together. He felt he was missing something crucial.

He accepted Laura's pushiness, understanding her ambitious drive for a movie production, and was willing to help jumpstart her acting career, but he wasn't going to do it alone. He took his laptop and studied the particular company he was interested in, verifying that nothing had changed.

Later that evening, Jake escorted Laura to Frank's restaurant.

"Do you want to eat first?" she asked.

"Yes, I'm hungry."

"Me too."

They ordered lobster and Jake passed on the liquor, not even wanting wine with his meal and opted for water while Laura had white wine. After they had eaten, they left the table and met Frank at the bar. Situated at the far corner for privacy, Jake took a seat while Laura stood beside Frank.

"You wanted to talk to me?" Frank asked.

"It's about the movie project."

"Of course, Laura's movie."

"I have a proposition for you. It's been mentioned that five hundred thousand is needed to get the project started, but overall it would be approximately a one to two million dollar production."

Frank listened.

"Here's the deal, we go in together. I will put up half a million if you do the same. It should get the movie well on its way."Laura studied Jake while he stayed focused on Frank.

"You want me to put up half a million to match your investment?"

"I have a plan. There is a company I've been following for some time. I've made small investments, and each one has turned a profit. I think if we both invest five hundred thousand dollars, we will double that amount. We get back our initial investment and make one million between us for Laura."

Jake glanced at Laura while Frank pondered the idea.

"Are you sure about this company?"

"I am."

Though Jake had made money on small investments, this would be the largest, and if it didn't occur as planned, he could lose it all. It was a huge risk, but one he felt confident would pay. He wanted to take a more aggressive approach to investing, and he figured why not start with acquiring cash for the movie. He'd like to see Laura get her production.

Frank thought about it, and glanced at Laura. She knew to remain silent.

"I can trust you on this?" Frank asked.

"I'm investing as much as you."

Frank looked at Jake straight in the eye.

"We'll do it, I'll call my advisor. Meet me at Laura's place at ten."

"I'll have the information by then," Jake said.

Frank put his arm around Laura's shoulder and drew her in for a hug.

"Well, Babe, looks like you're going to be in the movies," he told her.

"Jake, we'll talk in the morning. I need to get back to my customers," he said, reaching out to shake hands.

"I'll leave you two to celebrate. Joe, take care of them," Frank told the bartender.

Frank walked away. Laura threw herself at Jake, and wrapped her arms around his neck and kissed him.

"Thank you," she told him.

She sat on the barstool next to him. Joe took their order for drinks, and Laura lifted her glass for a toast.

"To money," she said.

"To your movie," Jake countered.

"Yes, to the movie."

They clicked glasses.

"I wasn't so sure you were interested in the project."

"I don't like to make hasty decisions."

"Well, you gave this one some thought. I'm so glad you're on board, we'll make a good team."

Jake played with his glass.

"I can't wait to call Evan and give him the good news. Finally, 'The Outer Eclipse' will be a movie."

"So that's the name of it."

"Yes."

"Interesting title."

"Let's go back to your place and celebrate," she said with a seductive smile.

Jake swallowed the remaining liquor, and they left the restaurant. He felt Laura was as emotionally involved in him as he was in her, and the night was in celebration.

Chapter 27

William and Seth were standing in the middle of one of their cornfields. Forty-five days and no rain was a disaster waiting to happen for any farmer, the ground was brittle. Seth stooped down and shifted the soil, stirring up dust.

"We've got to get water out here, or there'll be nothing left. I'm going to see about renting some extra water tanks. We can't stand by and do nothing."

William looked out over the land and couldn't imagine not having a legacy to leave his boys. He had prayed for rain, but it wasn't forthcoming. Seth was waiting for a response.

"Dad, we have to do something," he said with deliberation.

"I know, see what you can do to get the tanks. We won't be able to save it all, but some is better than none," he told him with a deep sigh.

They went to the house.

"We need to locate some water tanks," Seth told Mrs. Grey when entering the office.

She looked up from her work, and watched William go into his office and close the door.

"I'm on it," she said.

Seth went into Jake's office to make some inquiries. He grabbed the phone book and started going through the yellow pages. Three hours later between the two of them, they had six full tankers being delivered in the morning.

Mrs. Grey stood in the doorway where Seth was sitting behind Jake's desk.

"Now that we have the tanks, where are we going to get the water?" she asked.

"The tanks will be filled with water."

"I know that, but it will be gone in no time, and then what?"

Seth looked at her wishing he knew.

"See if the companies supplying the tanks will run containers of water out here on an ongoing basis."

"That's a long shot."

"I know, but we have to try."

William was sitting in one of the chairs in front of his desk when Seth barged into the office, and took the opposite seat.

"We've got six full tanks coming in the morning. Mrs. Grey is checking to see if they'll provide continuous shipments of water."

"That'll cost us. We don't have the money to pay for an ongoing supply of water," William told him.

"We do, I've already told you how we can cover these expenses."

William didn't respond. He knew what Seth was referring to.

"Did you check to see if the wells can be primed?" William asked.

"I thought of that a month ago, both are dried up. They haven't been used in years."

"It was a thought," William said.

"I know."

"Whether you are willing to admit it or not, we need to use some of my inheritance. Eventually it will rain, but in the meantime, we have to save what we can. Consider it a loan, whatever you want to call it, but we need that money, now."

Seth didn't give his father the opportunity to respond and left the office. On his way out the front door, he gave Mrs. Grey further instructions.

"We'll need some field workers in the morning to drive the tanks. Call in about twenty men."

"You got it."

It would be like watering a flower garden with a teaspoon, but an effort had to be made. Seth needed to make sure the two tanks they owned still worked, and the lines weren't plugged.

"I'll be in the barn, if you need me," he told her.

After charging the batteries and pouring diesel fuel in the tanks, both machines fired up. Seth let them idle for a while before changing the oil and filters, then added air to the tires, thankful there weren't any leaks. He backed them out of the barn, and left them idling. He went in search of the long water sprinkler extensions, and one by one laid them on the ground until he had two very long pipelines, for each side of the tanks.

He dragged the garden hose from the side of the barn across to the machines and began running water through both sprinkler lines to make sure the holes weren't clogged. Then he positioned the hose inside the tank and opened the water valve full force. Filling the tanks from the main line would create a huge water bill, but Seth wasn't concerned. He was out until dusk getting things ready, and hoped to salvage whatever he could.

First thing the next morning a caravan of three semi-trucks carrying two water tanks each was coming down the driveway. William and Seth were in the kitchen finishing breakfast when they heard the commotion. Seth was first out the front door with William lagging behind holding a second cup of coffee. Seth had it under control, so he watched from the porch as they unloaded the machinery. He sure hoped this worked.

Chapter 28

Jake rechecked the company stock, and there were no changes which was a good sign. He created a separate account for Frank to wire money into, and was ready to transfer his funds also, with the investment being made from this mutual account. The next morning, they met in Laura's apartment as planned.

"Good morning, Jake," Frank said as he entered the kitchen.

"Frank."

"How are you this morning, Laura?" Jake asked.

"I couldn't be better, I'm so excited."

"Should we do some business?" Frank asked.

"I've created a new account that we both can put our share into. Once the account reflects the funds, I'll buy the stock," Jake said, explaining.

"When will we get our return on the investment?"

"It can take a day or two, so we wait."

"Let's do it," Frank said.

Jake had brought his laptop and placed it on the kitchen counter. Once he was at the site, he pulled up the account while Frank called his financial advisor, Larry, on the cellphone.

"Got it," Jake said.

"Give me the account number."

Frank spoke with Larry, giving him instructions. When he ended the call, Jake was the first to speak.

"You won't regret it."

"I'm sure I won't. Larry will transfer the money. Said it could take a few hours because of the amount, something about getting bank clearance."

"I'll keep an eye on the account, and when the money is there, I'll make the purchase."

"Keep me informed."

"Let's celebrate," Jake said.

"You celebrate, I've got another appointment this morning. Jake, good doing business with you," Frank told him, extending his hand to shake Jake's.

"Same here, Frank."

"Laura, I'll see you later."

She followed Frank to the door but before leaving, he turned and winked at her. When she returned to the kitchen, Laura saw Jake punching keys, and made herself a fresh cup of coffee. When Jake was finished, he closed the laptop.

"It's been a busy morning," she said.

"A profitable one," he replied.

"Thank you, Jake, for doing this for me."

"How could I not help you get established in your acting?"

"I kind of pressure you a bit," she told him, teasingly.

"You did, but I agree that this is a win-win for both of us. I get my money back, and the profit that I make will go for your movie project."

"We can't lose," she said.

"No way, this is a sure thing."

"Let's throw a party and celebrate. This will be my big break playing the principal role, and I want to share it will all my friends."

"Aren't you just a bit worried that we might be premature in celebrating?"

"No, I trust you."

"Okay, let's have your party."

"How about your apartment, tomorrow night?"

"That's fast. Why not your place since they're your friends?"

"Your apartment is much larger than mine. A few phone calls, and I can have everyone here at six. They will bring snacks, and all the liquor we can imagine. You won't need to do anything."

"I see you've done this a few times."

"In my circle, someone is always throwing a party."

"Fine, tomorrow night, six, my place."

145

"Great, I'll make those calls, and see you later this afternoon," she told him.

He grabbed his laptop, and walked to the door with Laura following behind. When he turned, she slipped her arms around his neck and kissed him.

"Thank you."

"Your welcome."

He went to his apartment. There was nothing he needed to do but wait for the money transfers into the new account. Maybe a party wasn't such a bad idea, he thought. Jake decided to go to Siesta expecting to see Summer. He stepped in line and when his turn, ordered a dark roast coffee.

"No latte, today?"

"Just coffee."

"With a tad of cream," she said.

"Yes."

"How have you been?" Summer asked.

"Good."

"You seem excited about something."

"I'm pumped. Add a cinnamon bun to that order."

"You got it."

Jake paid and walked away from the counter. It was a busy morning with others standing behind him. He took a seat at a table near the window. A few minutes later, Summer brought his order.

"So what has made you so happy?"

"Making money," he told her.

"Of course."

"Must have hit the jackpot."

"That's the plan."

"When will you know for sure?"

"I would say within twenty-four hours, or so."

"I hope it works out for you."

"Oh, it will."

"You seem very sure of yourself, it's still a gamble."

"I know what I'm doing."

He was in such a positive mindset to be affected by her skepticism.

"I wasn't implying that you didn't."

"Let's have lunch today, I feel like celebrating."

"Isn't that a bit premature?"

"I don't think so. Do you want to join me for lunch?"

"Sure, but I don't get a break for two hours."

"I can be back at noon," he told her.

"Okay."

Summer went behind the counter while Jake sipped on his coffee, watching the passersby outside. When he was finished, he took off strolling along the sidewalk, peering into the neighboring shops and went inside one novelty store when a figurine in the display caught his attention.

He looked around but came back to the item. It was a colorful fabric butterfly resting atop a ceramic lily pad. The delicacy of it made him think of Summer, and he decided to buy it for her. Though not an expensive gift, it seemed to suit her. Jake went back to Siesta to meet with Summer, and they left the cafe.

"Are there any other eateries in this area besides the deli?" he asked.

"Three blocks down on the right is a restaurant, but they cater to business luncheons and are more pricey."

"Perfect, let's go there."

"Are you sure, a sandwich is fine."

"No, I want to take you somewhere special today."

She looked at him puzzled.

They walked to a place called Melvin's Grill. It was formal inside with the tables covered in clothe and small floral centerpieces. They were seated and the hostess handed them a menu.

"Have you been here before?" Jake asked.

"No."

"Good, a first for both of us."

They perused the menus, but Summer didn't know what to order.

"Do you know what you want?" he asked.

"Everything looks good."

"I'm having the salmon," he told her.

"The grilled chicken Alfredo sounds good, I'll have that."

The waitress came to their table with a pitcher of water, filled their glasses, and took their order. After she left, Jake placed a small gift bag on the table in front of Summer.

"What is this?"

She looked at him and frowned.

"Did you buy me something?"

"Take a look."

Summer pulled out the tissue paper. Wrapped in more tissue was a small figurine, and lifted it out of the bag and unwrapped it.

"This is so adorable," she told him, lightly touching the wing of the butterfly with her index finger.

Her face lit up.

"Why did you do this?"

"I saw it in a window display, and made me think of you."

"That is so sweet, I love it. Thank you."

He watched her rewrap the gift and place it in the bag then set it beside her purse.

"Are you going to tell me about this big investment that has you so happy?"

"Not much to tell, just a company I have been following for a while."

"More video games?"

"No, board games. They have a new one on the market and sales are good."

"I can see where that would be important."

"A good indicator of their stocks."

"What do you do with all this money you make?"

"I reinvest it."

"In the same stock, or different ones?"

"Sometimes in stocks, other times in outside ventures."

"What does that mean?"

"Well, I'm working on a movie project."

"How do you find these opportunities?"

"I pick up information."

"It's impressive, but still it would worry me to think I could lose the money just as easily. I wouldn't be good at it, but I'm glad for you."

The food arrived, and the remainder of lunch was on small talk. Summer talked about school, homework assignments, and some of her teachers as Jake listened. He realized Summer was easy to be around. She hadn't mentioned attending church, or bible study groups, and he was thankful for that.

The hour break went by quickly, and Jake walked her back to Siesta.

"Thanks for the lunch, and the gift."

"It wasn't much."

"It was very thoughtful. I've got to go inside."

"I'll see you later for that cup of coffee," he said, teasing her.

She smiled, leaving him standing on the sidewalk. He walked back to his apartment with a grin on his face. Life was good.

Jake checked his account and both his and Frank's money transfers were deposited. Sitting on the sofa with the laptop on the coffee table, he rubbed his hands together in anticipation, rechecked the stock, and with the stroke of a few keys, the purchase was made. He leaned back and stared at the screen, now it was a matter of waiting. This time tomorrow, he and Frank will have one million dollars each. Not bad, he thought.

Later that evening, he and Laura went to Frank's for their own private celebration. They took their time savoring the meal, and sipping on wine with Laura enthralled about the movie. Much of the conversation centered on the project, and Jake listened attentively understanding her excitement, for he felt the same way about his own profession. Frank eventually made an appearance at their table.

"Jake, how's it going, any news?"

"Won't know anything until tomorrow, at the earliest, these things take time."

"Let me know when you hear something. I'll see you later, babe," he said to Laura.

Jake didn't like the implication of his comment, but shrugged it off. They stayed at Frank's moving from the table to the bar, and continued drinking for several hours.

"I think it's time to call it a night," he told her.

"Sure, I'm ready too."

When they arrived at the apartment complex and entered the elevator, Jake pressed one button to the seventh floor thinking Laura would be joining him; however, she reached over and pressed number four.

"Aren't you coming to my place?"

"Not tonight, but I'll see you at the big party tomorrow. We'll have all night long to celebrate," she said, and kissed him.

Satisfied, Jake accepted her reasoning.

"True, we'll party the night away."

"That's the plan, need to rest up," she said, flirting.

"Got it."

The elevator opened and she kissed him again before walking out. Jake went to his apartment feeling confident that he and Laura were a solid couple. He was looking forward to her movie, and imagined being on the set watching her perform.

Chapter 29

The next day, Jake stayed in his apartment repeatedly checking his laptop, anxious for news. He wasn't in the mood for small talk with Summer, and he didn't expect to see Laura until later in the day. With time to waste, he flipped through cable stations on the television but nothing held his attention.

He decided to make a trip to the local liquor store for bottles of whiskey, scotch, vodka, and wine. Thought it might look good to have some available for the party. Next, he went to the grocery store to buy some chips, crackers, and packaged cubed cheese. He wondered what Laura was doing, but didn't inquire knowing they would be together the entire evening.

The day crept along and finally by four o'clock, he showered and readied for the party. Laura showed up at five and helped him set out trays of crackers and cheese, bowls of chips, and lined the liquor neatly on the kitchen counter. She brought an ice bucket and filled it with ice cubes.

"This will be fun," she told him.

Guests started arriving promptly at six, and the apartment was quickly becoming crowded. Jake recognized several of the people from Evan's party, along with some newcomers. Evan came with a couple of friends.

"We need some music," Laura said.

Jake turned on the stereo, put in a collection of his compact disks, playing a variety of artists.

"Is Frank coming?"

"No, he doesn't like parties."

"But this one is for you."

"Not his style, besides you and I are doing our own celebrating tonight, we don't need Frank."

Strangers kept showing up, and Jake counted approximately twenty-five people. Everyone was laughing, drinking, roaming throughout his place much to his discomfort.

"Relax, no one is going to break anything," Laura said, seeing he was uptight.

"You're right, it's a party, supposed to be having fun."

"That's the idea."

"Make us some drinks, and let's go mingle. There are some friends I want you to meet that weren't at Evan's party."

Jake made two scotch-on-the-rocks, and handed one to Laura. She took his hand and led him into the living room. As the night progressed, Jake realized that Laura's friends were professional partiers. It didn't take long for everyone to settle in and start downing the liquor. He was glad to see Laura laughing and enjoying herself, but as time passed, everyone was getting drunk including himself. Bodies were sprawled over sofas, chairs, and on the floor.

Laura dragged him to one corner of the sofa, put their drinks on the coffee table, and pulled him down beside her, turning to kiss him. Jake felt the rush from the alcohol, already completely intoxicated by her. He held her close while they continued to kiss.

"Great party," she said, tipsy.

"Tonight is all about you, Babe," he told her, deliberating using Frank's pet name.

"Kiss me," she cooed.

Jake placed his hands on either side of her head and drew her lips to his, kissing her passionately. Neither cared about their surroundings, so caught up in each other, and they weren't the only ones.

"Hey, Jake," a man called out from the kitchen.

It took him a moment to recognize his name.

"What?" he yelled.

"Man, I think someone just puked in your dishwasher, it's nasty. Do you want me to run it?"

"Turn it on the heavy cycle, pots and pans," he hollered, uninterested.

"Got it."

Laura drew his attention back to her.

A few blocks down the street, Summer was ending her shift, ready to leave for the university, when Mr. Foster walked in and motioned her to the end of the counter.

"Have you seen today's paper?"

"No, why?"

"There is something on the front page you might want to take a look at," he said, opening the paper and handing it to her.

"Is that your young man's family?"

Summer saw the picture, and began reading the short article about a drought in the Midwest, and showed a picture of the Abraham farm with a family photo of Jake, his father, and brother.

"They could lose everything."

"I wonder if he's seen the paper," he said.

Summer looked up.

"Can I have this?"

"Of course."

"I have to go, talk to you later."

Summer removed her apron and left the cafe. She knew the building Jake lived in, and ran the several blocks to his complex. Upon entering the lobby, she saw a list of the residents by floor, found his name with the apartment number, and pressed the button to his apartment. A guest hearing a voice over the intercom system pressed a button causing the elevator to open and she rushed in. The music from his apartment became louder as she approached his door. When no one answered her knocking, she pounded on the door and a stranger opened to let her in.

The apartment was crowded, loud, and everyone was intoxicated. At first, Summer didn't see Jake, but as she weaved her way further into the room, she spotted him on the sofa with a blonde woman. She walked up and threw the paper at him, and Jake looked to see her standing there.

"You might want to read the front page," she said, disgusted, and turned to walk out.

Jake called after her, but she rushed through the people and out the door. He untangled himself from Laura and opened the newspaper to see the picture of his family with the headline, "Drought Destroying Farms in Midwest".

"What is it, Jake?" Laura asked, noticing the sudden change in him.

"Nothing."

He got up taking the newspaper with him into the bedroom only to find a woman passed out across his bed. Jake sat on the edge, and opened the nightstand drawer removing his grandfather's watch, rubbing the surface with his thumb. He thought of the day his father handed it to him, and bowed his head, disheartened by the news.

"Dad," he said aloud, before placing the watch back in the drawer.

He stepped onto the bedroom balcony, and the cool evening air helped to clear his head. It bothered him to know the farm was in jeopardy. When he walked back through the bedroom into the living room, he heard Laura's laughter. She was talking with a man across the room, and as he drew near to join her, Jake overheard the conversation.

"If we can get a lead investor to put up just a little bit of the money to show other investors that someone believes in the movie, then others will follow. You'll be on board, it's not a lot of money, just enough to break the ice."

"I take it you want me to be that lead investor," the man replied. "You can be the one in charge of the other investors because you would be first," she tells him, flirting.

The man smiled at her. Laura placed her right hand on his arm, and leaned in seductively.

"It would be worth it," she told him, lowering her voice and smiling up at him.

The implication was unmistakable. Jake stopped in his tracks, shocked. He couldn't believe what he just witnessed. He wanted to walk up, grab her, and confront her, but he didn't want to cause a scene. Instead, Jake went out onto the living room balcony, and leaned against the railing. He felt sick and wasn't sure if it was the news of the farm, the disappointment he saw in Summer's eyes, or Laura's crushing blow. He believed he and Laura had something special, and even though she was intoxicated, he realized it wasn't the first time she had played this role.

It took Laura a while to come looking for him, he noted, obviously not missing his presence. In some ways, he was glad because he didn't know what to say to her.

"Jake, what are you doing out here?"

"Getting some air."

"Are you alright?"

"No, I'm not. Can we call off the party? I'm done for the night."

"Why? Everyone is having such a good time. What happened to you earlier? What was that newspaper about?" she asked, standing beside him.

"Nothing."

"It must be something, you jumped off the sofa. Where's the paper?"

"It's not important."

"Come on back to the party, the night is still young."

She reached for his hand, but he withdrew.

"Jake, what is it? You are acting strange."

"I said, I want to call off the party."

She watched him.

"Fine."

Laura left him in search of Evan to help spread the word that they needed to leave. Couples started filing out of the apartment and once everyone was gone, Laura found Jake still on the balcony.

"The party has been moved to Evan's house."

Jake didn't care where they went.

"Well, this wasn't the big celebration I expected."

He turned and looked at her.

"I'm not feeling well, let's call it a night."

"Sure, no problem, I'll see you tomorrow."

Laura walked to the front door without glancing back. Jake witnessed the mess in his apartment, then went to the bedroom, thankful someone remembered the woman. He sat on the edge of the bed leaning forward with his head in his hands, deeply saddened and hurt. He felt betrayed.

Chapter 30

Everything was crashing in on him. Apparently Laura had been lying the entire time, and it hurt too much to think he had been used. His thoughts migrated to Summer, and the appalled look on her face when she saw a woman sprawled on top of him, and the raunchy party in his apartment. What must she be thinking, he wondered. She wasn't likely to forget the scene. His thoughts drifted to his father, and he debated calling, but there was nothing he could do about the drought.

After checking his investment, he took a walk to Siesta. Talking with Summer wouldn't be pleasant, but he didn't want to avoid her, and felt the need to explain. She saw him enter the cafe and walked away from the counter; however, realizing she had no choice but to serve him, she returned but didn't say anything.

"Aren't you supposed to ask me what I'm having?"

"What would you like to drink this morning, sir?"

"Sir, is it."

"I'll have a dark roast, no cream."

She sidestepped to the register."

"That will be three twenty-five."

He handed her a five dollar bill.

"Keep the change."

He left the counter and sat on the short sofa next to the window. Summer made his coffee and placed it on the low table in front of him without saying a word, and turned to leave.

"Summer," he called after her.

She looked at him.

"Is this the way it's going to be between us now?"

"There is no us."

"I thought we were becoming friends."

"So did I, but I was wrong. You had an apartment full of friends last night, you don't need one more."

"It's not like that, I didn't know those people."

"You could have fooled me."

"You've got it all wrong."

"Do I? My eyes were not deceived. We don't hang around the same type of people."

"I told you they're not my friends."

She sat down.

"You know, I thought you were a nice guy, but after what I witnessed, I'm not so sure. You don't have to live your life like this."

"What are you talking about?"

"You came here to make something of yourself."

"I am," he told her, bewildered by her attitude.

"Are you?"

"You know, I really don't see how any of this is your business."

"I thought…"

He cut her off.

"No, don't think you can change me, or make me a better person somehow. I'm fine on my own. Do you understand?" he asked her, sternly.

"I get it."

She paused.

"Why did you leave home?"

"What?"

"Obviously, the family business is in jeopardy. Why aren't you with your family?"

"Are we changing the subject?"

"I read the article."

"Since when did you become my keeper?" he asked, irritated.

"I'm not."

"Glad you know that."

"I'm just trying to understand why you are here, and not with them."

Jake couldn't believe her directness.

"I'm still not following when my life became your concern."

"You're here in the city making your big bucks while your father and brother are struggling and could lose everything, but you're right, it's not my business."

"You know, I came in this morning to make amends for yesterday, but I can see you aren't interested."

Ignoring his statement, Summer continued, upset.

"I didn't take you for a two-timing, cold-hearted jerk, but obviously, I was mistaken."

The conversation escalated again.

"Wait a minute. You don't know anything about me, or my family."

"I know enough that they are having a hard time, and you're here partying."

The conversation was over.

"I've got to go."

Jake stood up and Summer watched him leave. He passed Mr. Foster at the entrance without saying a word to him.

Summer was angry and hurt. Seeing Jake in the middle of a wild party wasn't what she expected of him. She knew her words were harsh, but it was the way she felt. Maybe it wasn't her place to be so outspoken, but she thought they were becoming friends, and wanted to help him. Now she may never know if there could have been more between them.

She went to the counter to make Mr. Foster's coffee, and joined him for a moment.

"Your friend didn't look too happy."

"We got into an argument, and I said some hurtful things."

"He'll come around. He's a grown man and has to live by his convictions, whether they be good, or not so good."

"I was beginning to really like Jake, but I've discovered he's not the kind of person I want to be with."

"If it's meant to be, it will be. God will see to that."

"We weren't very nice to each other."

"Things have a way of working out."

She left the table and went behind the counter as business was picking up. Summer didn't think she would see Jake again. He had another woman in his life, and probably would find another place to get his morning coffee.

Jake walked in the opposite direction of his apartment at a fast pace. A few blocks away, he sat on a vacant bench and thought about what Summer had said. He didn't like the idea that she thought he was a jerk, that stung. What did she expect him to do? He knew she cared about him and was trying to interject her thoughts to help, but it wasn't what he wanted to hear. Once he calmed down and could think clearly, he understood her compassion, accepting the truth in what she said, but it didn't change the fact that it was his life, and no one was telling him how to live it.

He knew how much the farm meant to his father and the prospect of losing it would be devastating. Jake also accepted that his presence would not help the situation because it was rain they were in need of. It bothered him, but he had more pressing matters to concentrate on.

Jake went back to the condo to check on the investment, but still no news. He was grateful for hiring a cleaning service through the recommendation of Sandra to clean the mess from the party. For the first time, he had no interest in Laura and reconciled himself to the reality that she had done this many times with many men. Jake still wondered about Frank.

Chapter 31

Jake's cellphone was set to signal for incoming messages, and when he heard the bell, he grabbed the phone beside him on the sofa. He jumped up reading the text, and rushed to the dining room table to his laptop.

"What? No. No...no...no," he said, aloud.

Disturbed by the news, he opened the laptop and punched keys on the keypad.

"This can't be happening. Due to irregularities in Fischer and Bate's earnings report, the Securities and Exchange Commission froze trading on all stock in this company," he read.

"No, that's not possible."

Jake picked up the cellphone in frustration and made a call, but couldn't get through. He paced the apartment, attempting again to contact the SEC to gain further information. He's sidetracked when he heard a knock on the door, and disconnected the call putting the phone in his pocket. He opened the door to see Laura.

"Come on in," he said, upset.

Jake walked into the living room with a worried expression on his face, unbeknown to Laura following behind.

"I've phoned my producer, and I wanted to talk to you about investing more money, enough to cover some additional expenses."

Still talking to his back, she realized he wasn't responding.

"Hey, what's going on? What's wrong with you?"

Jake turned and looked at her. He was so distraught, he blurted it out.

"It's gone."

"What are you talking about?"

"The money is gone."

She was shocked.

"What do you mean?"

"They lied. The company we invested our money in lied to the SEC about how much capital they had on hand. They artificially inflated their assets so they could use the company's stocks to borrow against, and that way they would have enough money to continue manufacturing."

"What are you talking about?"

"I'm talking about a fraudulent misrepresentation of their holdings, and the government found out about it."

"So."

"Don't you understand, they lied, the company lied. The assets, the stocks, everything to do with this company has been frozen by the SEC which means we own shares that are worthless. We can't do anything with them. We can't share them, we can't trade them, and we can't sell them. They have absolutely no value and just sitting in the account, doing nothing. It will take a lawsuit for us to get our money back."

"How long will it take?"

"Months, years maybe, who knows. Even then, we may only recoup pennies on the dollar, we're toast."

Angrily, she pointed a finger at him.

"No, you're toast. Frank made this investment on your recommendation," she said, raising her voice.

"He knew it was a risk, you can't hold that against me."

"Do you know what an idiot you've made me look like in front of all my friends, telling them we're going forward with this movie project. You're disgusting," she yelled at him.

"Settle down, all we have to do is think of a new plan."

"No, I don't know if you've noticed, but there is no more we," she told him, storming out of his apartment.

Jake let out a deep sigh, not knowing what to do. Everything he had made in the past couple of months was part of the investment that went sour. He checked his online account to see if any funds were left to reinvest and make some money, fast, but there wasn't enough to buy any stocks. He sat down on the sofa and closed his eyes realizing within five months, he had blown a million dollars, including his recent earnings. It just wasn't possible, he thought. No one could have known the company he so carefully investigated would put false information in the market.

Jake decided to leave Laura alone for a few hours giving her time to cool off, and planned to stop by her apartment later. He checked his wallet for money and found a twenty dollar bill, and went to an ATM machine to withdrew from his personal bank account which gave him eighty dollars. The printout slip showed a balance of thirteen dollars and seven cents which he shoved into his pocket. There had to be a way to get some quick cash and reinvest. He knew he could make the money, and went back to the apartment complex and knocked on Laura's door. She opened it but didn't invite him in.

"What do you want?"

"We need to talk."

"No, we don't. You need to leave."

"We can fix this, but it will take time. I need you to understand, this isn't my fault."

"Then who's is it. Frank and I trusted you. All the people involved in the movie project trusted you to come through."

"I don't care about your movie right now. I need Frank to lend me some cash, so I can invest and make some money."

She laughed.

"You want me to ask Frank to give you money. Are you insane?"

"Just a small amount."

"You'd better leave before Frank finds out he's lost half a million dollars. He will be livid to hear this."

"You aren't going to help me, are you?"

"Leave, Jake, and don't come here again."

"What we had together meant nothing to you?" he asked.

He couldn't believe she would cut him off like this.

"We didn't have anything."

Jake left the building, not caring where he went. After walking a considerable distance, he came upon a park and sat under a tree. He needed money to start over, but didn't know where to get it. Jake found it hard to accept that Laura wouldn't help him, and thought she was just too upset to think clearly. He called her.

Laura's cellphone rang and several seconds later, she hit the talk button.

"Jake."

"I know you're mad at me, but have you seen Frank?"

"He thinks you lied about everything."

"What? I didn't."

"It doesn't matter. He's out half a million dollars because of you, and he's coming for his money."

"I don't have it. I lost money too," he told her, upset.

"Frank only cares about his investment. He's angry and looking for you. A word of warning, if he finds you, he'll kill you."

Jake ignored her comment.

"Tell him I need time and some cash, and I can get his money back."

"Frank trusted you, and you let him down. He isn't a patient man."

Jake couldn't believe this.

"Tell him he can have the condo and the car, I'll leave the keys for him."

"Jake, that's not going to work. I don't think you understand the severity of the situation. Frank doesn't want your leftovers, he wants money. You better come up with the cash and fast."

"How am I going to do that if I don't have any money to reinvest? He'll listen to you, convince him that I'm good for it."

She paused before answering.

"I'll talk to him, but don't expect anything. I suggest you disappear."

"I'll call you later," Jake said, worried.

Laura hung up.

With his elbows on his knees, he held his head in his hands. He had to think of a way to get some cash. He was confident that if he had money, he could get back what he lost. Surely, Laura was exaggerating that Frank would kill him, he thought.

Chapter 32

Jake walked back towards his apartment thinking of what he had as collateral, remembering the condominium. If he couldn't trade it off to Frank, perhaps he could get some cash for it and went to Strutton and Associates hoping to find Sandra in her office, and walked in unannounced.

"Mr. Abraham," Sandra said, looking up from her desk.

"I need some cash."

"Excuse me. You are in the wrong place, we're not a bank."

"No, you don't understand," he said, flustered.

"I want to withdraw the down payment I made on the condominium."

"I'm sorry, but I can't change the contract."

"I need that money. Isn't there anyway to make the down payment less, and add the difference to the monthly payments."

He was desperate.

"It doesn't work that way, and besides the deposit you made has already been paid to the previous owner. I don't have it."

She didn't know what his problem was, but was becoming uncomfortable with his desperation.

"Whatever has happened to you, I'm sorry. The only thing I can do to help is sell the unit, and that way you can recoup your money."

"That will take too long."

Jake thought for sure he could get something for the condo only to find it a complete loss, and left her office without saying another word. He was afraid to run into Frank at the apartment, and with nowhere else to go, he walked the distance to Siesta. It was late afternoon, and the place wasn't crowded.

"What happened to you?" Summer asked.

"You don't want to know."

"Give me a coffee and cinnamon bun."

Jake took out one of the twenties.

"That's five seventy-five, and change in the tip jar."

"No, I'll take that change."

"Of course."

She handed him his money, a bit surprised. Something was wrong.

Jake went to sit at a table in the far corner away from the front window. He didn't want to be seen. Summer brought his coffee and bun to the table.

"You don't look good."

He took a sip of the coffee.

"I'm not."

"Why do I feel something bad has happened? Is it your family?" she asked, sitting down.

He paused for a moment, deciding to be truthful.

"I lost it."

"I don't understand."

"I lost the money."

"What are you talking about, an investment?"

He could barely look at her.

"Yes."

"How much?"

He took another swig of the coffee, and bit into the cinnamon bun. Summer patiently waited for him to speak. He looked away for a minute, and then back at her.

"Half a million."

"Oh my gosh, Jake, no," she said, shocked.

"Can you reinvest and get it back?"

"It takes money to do that, and I don't have any left."

"Jake, I'm so sorry. Don't take this the wrong way, but you know, the investments always were a risk," she said, attempting to gently remind him.

"That's not what I need to hear right now."

He downed the last of the coffee, and stood up.

166

"What are you going to do?"

"I have to make some money."

He went to the door, turned and looked at her before opening it.

"I'm sorry things weren't different between us."

Jake pushed the door wide open and joined the passersby on the sidewalk. Summer watched him through the window until he disappeared into the crowd. She felt bad for Jake, but there wasn't anything she could do to help him, except to pray.

Counting on Frank being at his restaurant since it was the dinner hour, Jake went to his apartment. When the elevator door opened, he saw Frank standing at his door, and raced for the emergency stairway and ran down seven flights, flying out the side door of the complex into an alley. He continued to run until he caught up with the busy sidewalk crowd moving towards the downtown area, and stopped at the Lincoln Plaza Hotel. Seeing he wasn't followed, Jake entered the lobby, located a discrete corner chair, and plopped down.

He breathed heavily while resting his head on the back of the chair. The reality of Laura's words hit him hard because he was now fleeing for his life, and it frightened him. Jake had to think of a way to pay Frank, or else he would always be running and looking over his shoulder. He thought of all his assets, remembering the Maserati.

Surely, the dealership would take it back. Feeling somewhat better for having a plan, Jake waited until nearly midnight believing Frank would be at his restaurant with Laura. He carefully walked back to the condo glancing often over his shoulder. After taking the stairs to the seventh floor, he opened the door and peeked around the corner to find the hallway clear, ran to his apartment, tested to verify it was still locked, then unlocked it and went in.

He rushed to the bedroom, grabbed his suitcase and duffel bag from the closet, and threw them on the bed. Hurriedly tossing his clothes and toiletries in them, and moving to the dining room, got his laptop and shoved it into the duffel bag. Jake quickly headed for the door with bags in hand. While reaching for the doorknob, he saw the expensive watch on his wrist, remembered his grandfather's and raced back into the bedroom, opened the nightstand drawer and retrieved the watch, squeezing it in the palm of his hand for a second. He pulled the fancy one off his wrist, dropped it in the duffel bag and shoved his grandfather's into his pants pocket.

Jake ran out of the apartment taking the stairs, went to his car parked in the complex garage, threw his stuff in, and pulled into traffic driving out of town. He didn't have enough cash for a cheap hotel room, hoping to find a vacant lot and sleep in the car until morning, when he could sell it back to the dealership. He had been running all day on adrenaline and a cinnamon bun, when he saw a sign advertising a twenty-four hour diner just outside the city limits, and parked in front. Even though he had not ventured into this area of the city, and a quick glance showed it to be very unfavorable, Jake wasn't concerned for all he wanted was a sandwich before being on his way.

He got out of the car and walked inside taking a seat at the counter, placing the key in front of him. There weren't too many patrons this time of night. The waitress came over to greet him, and he ordered a tuna sandwich and coffee without looking at the menu. He noticed two scary looking men with long straggly hair watching him from the back corner, and it made him nervous.

When the plate of food arrived, he nonchalantly slid the key to one side and took a bite of the sandwich. The two men left their table and in passing behind Jake, one tripped and fell forward. Jake glanced over his shoulder to see what happened, but made no effort to help as the man quickly stood, and nodded at Jake before walking out the door. As Jake took another bite of the sandwich, he heard the engine of the Maserati, and quickly turned in the seat looking through the window to see the two men backing away in his car. He reached for his key on the counter, but it was gone. Jake bolted out the door to see the man in the passenger seat wave at him with a big grin on his face and took off running after them as fast as he could, screaming at the top of his lungs.

He stopped in the middle of the street out of breath and bent over resting his hands on his knees, then walked over to the curb and sat down in the blackness of night as there were no streetlights in this neighborhood. Everything he owned was in that car, and now it was gone, ending his chance to make some money. Jake didn't know where he was, or what to do. Scared and alone, he crossed his arms over bent knees and rested his head on his forearm unaware he was crying until he looked up, and felt the cool night air against the moisture on his cheeks. Jake pulled his jacket close around him and stood up to see an alley with a large dumpster and went behind it to hunker down for the night. He wouldn't give up on the idea that he could turn this around if only he had some money.

There was no way to predict that a company would defraud their shareholders causing them to lose their investments, and Jake his inheritance. He had carefully investigated this company and followed their market trend diligently. The one thing that should never have happened, did. Laura was upset with losing the movie opportunity, but surely she wouldn't hold that against him. Jake planned to call her in the morning and talk this through, believing she would be more rational.

Chapter 33

Jake needed a plan and spent most of the night awake, thinking. Though he no longer had his laptop, he was confident to get internet access in a library and connect to his online trading account and invest. All he needed to do was deposit money into his bank account through an ATM machine and transfer the funds. The problem was getting the cash. Laura had to have a few thousand dollars to lend him, or a friend like Evan she could borrow from, he thought.

He wasn't feeling any better for the circumstance he was in, but at least had a plan. In the early morning hours, Jake rested his head against the side of the dumpster falling asleep and awoke to the sound of a barking dog in the distance, something uncommon in the city. He stumbled to his feet and looked around, the street was quiet. Desperately needing a cup of coffee and hungry, he walked back to the diner remembering he ran out without paying for the sandwich. When he went inside, the diner was busier, and he took the same seat at the counter observing the same waitress was working.

Jake didn't think he would get served unless he proved he could pay for the meal, so he reached into his pocket, pulled out a twenty and placed it on the counter. She saw the money and came over.

"Sorry, I forgot to pay last night. I was distracted when my car was stolen," he told her.

"I saw that, no problem. We get that all the time, probably goes with the territory. If you haven't noticed, it's not the better part of town. You don't look like you're from around here."

"No, I was passing through."

"How about some coffee?" she asked.

"That's great."

She stepped away returning with a cup, and placed it in front of him.

"We have a breakfast special of two eggs, two bacon strips, homestyle potatoes, and a stack of pancakes for five ninety-five."

"Sounds good."

"Coming right up."

She walked away, but he called her back.

"Do you have a phone I can use, my cellphone is dead? I want to report the theft."

"Sure."

Jake dialed 911, and the dispatcher rerouted his call to the police department. They would send someone out.

Jake sipped on the coffee and watched the people in the diner. Most looked like shady characters at best, and they were eyeing him equally. He turned his attention to the waitress and asked her for a piece of paper and pen. She tore off a sheet from her pad and handed him a pen. Jake was thinking about the money he needed to ask of Laura for the number of shares to buy while contemplating which company would be the safest to invest in. He had to check their stocks first. Comfortable with a solid plan, he ate his breakfast. The twenty covered two meals with tips.

Two police officers walked into the diner, and Jake left the counter to sit in the booth. The waitress automatically brought two cups of coffee for the officers, and volunteered that she was a witness to the crime. Upon request, Jake furnished his drivers license and insurance card, and one of the men wrote down the information. He gave the condominium as his current residential address along with his cellphone number, explaining that he had yet to change the information on his license. He gave the make and model of the car which raised an eyebrow as they wondered how a young man could afford such an expensive vehicle.

Satisfied they had the details of the theft for their report and could obtain the vehicular license plate number from the state of Missouri, they left the diner informing Jake they would be in touch when they had news. They told him it could take time for in many cases of car thefts, especially expensive exotic cars, they are often sold out of state, out of country, or striped down for parts. It didn't sound encouraging that he would get his

Maserati back. Jake walked outside the diner with the officers, shook hands, and watched as they drove away.

He stood for a minute and slid his jacket sleeve up to see what time it was, and remembered his prized watch was in the duffel bag. Jake reached inside his pocket for his grandfather's watch, noticing it was too early to call Laura, concerned Frank was with her. He'd wait a bit longer, and began walking towards downtown which was a distance. After about an hour, Jake retrieved the cellphone from his pocket and speed-dialed her number, but it went to voicemail. He didn't leave a message, and kept on walking. Several times throughout the morning he attempted to reach her, but she wasn't answering, and he worried that she was avoiding him. He had to speak with her.

Jake kept calling her number throughout the day and knew with caller ID she was aware of his attempt to reach her. The battery power was down to two bars on his phone and had no charger, and not enough money to buy another one. If he could get to an electronics store, there might be a chance to recharge with a display, but he didn't know where a store was and couldn't wait even if he found one. His means of communication was nearly dead. He had spent the entire day walking, and looked around to find he was lost. The sun was setting, he was hungry, and fear was rising up within him. He stopped beneath an overpass and leaned against a graffiti-covered concrete wall to try calling Laura again. Punching the number, he listened to the rings. This time she answered.

"Laura, don't hangup, please."

"What do you want, Jake?"

"Just listen, and please don't hang up, okay," he said, desperate.

This was his last opportunity, his only hope.

"You've got five minutes, and then I am hanging up."

"I have a plan to get Frank's money back, but I need you to get me some cash, a few thousand dollars is all."

Jake paused, but when she doesn't respond, he continued.

"I can get the money back, but I need some cash to make an investment. You are the only one who can help me. You have to do this, Laura."

"No, Jake, I don't have to do anything."

"Please, Laura. I thought we had something special between us. I can't believe you wouldn't help me to turn this around, and make it right. I can do this, just give me a chance," he begged.

There was silence on the phone.

"Help me, please."

"Why should I? You've already made me look like a fool. My friends would surely laugh when they find out I helped you."

"Come on, you know I can do this, but I need your help. I need some money and a place to crash, maybe with one of your friends, someplace where Frank can't find me. In a few days, this can be behind us, and Frank will get his money."

Another pause.

"Alright."

Relieved, Jake let out an audible sigh.

"I'll call Evan, he'll do it for me. I'll talk to him, meet me at his place in an hour."

"I can't."

"You asked me to help you against my better judgment, and you tell me you can't meet me," she said, incredulous.

"Forget it."

"No, you don't understand, I don't have my car."

"Where is it?"

"It was stolen last night."

"How did it get stolen?"

"It's a long story, can you come get me?"

"Where are you?"

"I don't know," he said, looking around for a street sign, or something to identify his location.

Jake walked out from under the overpass, and saw a sign on the side.

"Hawthorne."

"What are you doing way over there? That's across town."

"Another long story. How long will it take you to get here?"

"Give me an hour."

"Thank you. You won't regret this, Laura. I promise you, I will make it up to you."

"You better," she told him.

Jake's phone is flashing. He had used the last battery power, and it went blank.

"Great."

He shoved it into his pocket to wait for Laura. He was completely out of options.

Chapter 34

Finally after months, it rained and there was hope for salvaging a decent yield. Seth succeeded in persuading his father to borrow against his portfolio which helped to sustain the business during the drought.

William and Seth stood on the porch watching the rain.

"Sure is a good sight," William said.

"We'll make it," Seth told his father.

"We always have."

"Dad, you need to call Sam."

"Let's hope he's willing to come back. It's been a month, and he may be employed."

"If that's the case, offer him a raise."

"I'll give him a call."

"Good."

They both went inside, and William into his office. He called Samuel to offer his old job, and Sam agreed to be there in the morning. Seth was standing in front of Mrs. Grey's desk when William walked out of his office.

"Sam will be here in the morning," he announced.

"Oh, that's good news," Mrs. Grey said, excited for his return.

"Great," Seth said.

William went back into his office, and sat down in one of the chairs. Things were turning around for the business as they always have by the grace of God, he knew. His thoughts drifted to Jake wondering what he was doing. Not one word from him since the day he drove off the property. It saddened William to think he may never see him again.

The next morning Sam was at the farm early, before William and Seth had finished breakfast, and knocked on the front office door. Seth went to answer it.

"Sam, good to see you, come on in. You didn't have to come out so early," Seth told him, shaking his hand.

"I figured there may be plenty for me to catch up on."

"Join us in the kitchen for some coffee."

"Thanks."

William saw Samuel following behind Seth, and stood to shake his hand. Seth poured a cup and handed it to him as he joined them at the table.

"I didn't mean to interrupt your breakfast."

"We're done," Seth said.

"How've you been?" William asked.

"I'm doing okay. Sure was glad to get your call."

"We're glad you're back," Seth told him.

"What's the plan for today?" Sam asked.

"All the equipment in both barns need a complete overhaul, and if there are any worn parts, replace them. We pulled the tankers out, so they should go back into storage."

Seth brought things to Samuel's attention knowing it would get done.

"Feels like old times," Sam said with a smile.

"Good to have you back, Sam. I'm going out to the barn. Meet me there when you finish your coffee."

"Right behind you."

Seth took his plate and cup to the sink and left the kitchen.

"Thank you for hiring me, again," Sam told him.

"Sam, I never should have let you go in the first place, that was poor judgment on my part."

"I don't have all the money from the severance package, but I brought the balance and will repay the remainder."

"Keep it."

Samuel was shocked.

"That wouldn't be right."

"That was the arrangement then. It doesn't apply to my rehiring you. I'll make sure your benefits are retroactive."

"That's very generous of you."

"The way I see it, we caused you a hardship, not intentional of course, but nonetheless."

"Thank you."

He stood and shook William's hand, took his cup to the sink, and went to meet Seth in the barn to begin his first day back on the farm. The fresh morning air still had the lingerings of rainfall, and things were back to normal, except for Jake not being with them.

Chapter 35

Jake waited for Laura to show up. It was dark and from his location under the bridge, he could see the outline of the downtown lights. Crouched down on the ground, he listened to the cars on the highway above him. About forty-five minutes later, Jake noticed the shadow of two men approaching him, and jumped to attention. As they came closer, he recognized Frank.

"Frank, these things happen," he began to explain as he drew near.

Before Jake could say another word, the other guy walked up, and punched him hard in the stomach. Jake doubled over in pain, having the breath knocked out of him.

"You made me chase you all over town. You made me chase you like some chump."

Frank grabbed the front of his jacket with both hands, and pulled him up.

Jake could barely speak.

"You can have my car, my condo, it's yours."

"I want my money, that's what I want. Do you hear me, take accountability. You've got one week, and don't even think of running because I'll find you."

Frank slapped him in the face before motioning to the guy.

"Tell him."

The guy hit him again in the stomach, and Jake fell to the ground. Frank pointed a finger at him.

"One week."

They left him lying there. Jake waited for the pain to subside before attempting to stand and leaned against the cement wall, then walked a short distance to a spot off the street to hide for the night. He curled up on the ground unable to sleep. He knew Frank meant business and would kill him if he didn't come up with the money, there was no place to hide. It was hard to accept that Laura turned him over to Frank. Even so, Jake couldn't let go of the thought that if he had some money all this could be corrected. He had to think harder.

He awoke to the sound of voices and froze as teenagers walked passed him probably skipping school. Jake waited for them to be gone before standing and in the daylight, he noticed a small shopping area and walked in that direction following the sidewalk into a gun shop. The clerk came up to him at the counter.

"What happened to you?"

"Long story."

"It usually is."

"I need a gun."

"Have you ever used one?"

"No."

"You've got to get trained, and know how to use it safely. You'll need to attend a weapons class and become certified."

"I don't have time for that, I need one today."

"Even if I sold you a gun today, there is a ten day waiting period before I can turn it over to you, it's the law."

Jake didn't have ten days, hoping he could trade his grandfather's watch. He pulled the watch from his pocket, and placed it on the glass top counter.

"Can I trade this for one?"

"We don't do trades here, we're not a pawn shop. Besides, that looks like a special watch, you should keep it."

"I don't have money."

"Then this isn't your lucky day. I can't take the watch as payment, and you still have to wait. There is no way you can walk out today with a gun. I'm sorry, but I can't help you," he said, stressing his point.

Jake put the watch in his pocket, and left the gun shop. He pulled the bills from his pocket and counted them while walking to the other end of the strip mall. With forty dollars to his name, Jake went inside a deli taking a seat in the back, and ordered a cup of coffee and a corn-beefed sandwich when the waitress came over. He leaned back on the bench resting his head and closed his eyes, listening to his stomach growl. Reality had caught up with him; no money, no collateral, and Frank was going to kill him in six days.

Jake stayed in the deli until they closed at four, and found another place to hide by nightfall. He hadn't bathed or shaved in days, and was looking like a homeless person. His week was up and Frank would be looking for him. As the days passed, there was no returning to the lifestyle he once had, and his remaining money was spent on hamburgers. He went to a fast food restaurant to buy a meal with the credit cards in his wallet, but the three he had were declined, and he left hungry.

Days drifted into weeks as he roamed the streets, having traveled on foot to another area of the city to avoid being discovered. Jake came upon a middle-aged man holding a cardboard sign on the corner of a busy street. As he came near, the man yelled at him.

"Get away, this is my corner."

Jake didn't know what to make of his instant hostility.

"What?"

"Don't you come any closer."

"I'm not going to hurt you," Jake said, confused.

"This is my place, you aren't going to take my money. Go find yourself another corner."

"I don't know what you're talking about, I don't want your corner."

The stranger watched Jake, unbelieving.

"Can you tell me where to find a YMCA?"

The man remained focused on Jake.

"Where do you spend your nights? Maybe I can go with you."

The nights were turning cold, and he had to find a place to stay. No longer feeling threatened, the man decided to help.

"When I'm finished here, you can come with me."

"Thanks."

Jake stood far enough away from him and didn't attempt to make conversation, nor did the stranger. Cars slowed and threw dollar bills out the window, but he didn't pick them up. As the sun was setting, the man folded his sign, and started walking without saying a word with Jake following a few steps behind.

They walked several blocks crisscrossing the streets and alleys before reaching an old faded red brick building with a sign on the front that read, "My Neighbor in Need". The man opened the door and went inside to a large room with a buffet of food at one end and tables and chairs with men of all ages eating. Jake continued to follow as he studied the room.

The stranger went to the buffet and took a tray helping himself to food while Jake stood watching. When he didn't take a tray, the man looked at him.

"It's free, if you're worried about paying for your meal, so grab a tray," he instructed, slightly friendlier.

Jake took a tray and stood in line filling his plate with home-cooked food along with an iced tea at the dispenser, and joined the man at an empty table, but hesitated to eat.

"What's wrong?" the stranger asked.

"Nothing."

"Then eat," he said, shoving food into his mouth.

"Where does this food come from?"

"People fulfill the needs of others anonymously through my neighbor in need."

"I saw that on the sign."

"It's true, strangers are helping strangers every day," he said, more conversationally.

"What kind of place is this?"

"A homeless shelter. You got a problem with that?"

"I don't know," Jake answered, frowning.

"I'd get over it fast if you want hot food and a bed to sleep in. Looks like you could use a shower too."

Jake slowly began eating a meal of chicken casserole with mixed vegetables. The man went over to the buffet table for a cup of coffee, and Jake mimicked his steps. While sitting at the table, the man watched Jake.

"What's your name?"

"Jake."

"I'm Al. Why aren't you working?"

Surprised by his question, Jake didn't know how to answer.

"Let me guess, you were on top of the world, rich and popular. I bet you have a college degree," he said, sarcastically.

"I do."

"Well, how about that, we've got ourselves a speller. Maybe you can help some of the boys with their signs."

He paused, and then continued.

"First piece of advice, your sob story isn't any better than anyone else in here, so don't think it will win you any sympathy."

"I never said that."

"Number two, don't panhandle at the gray house down the street, they're Canadian, takes forever to get rid of those quarters."

"Okay," Jake said, confused.

"Three, you need to have prepared answers for the two most common questions you'll get in here."

"What's that?"

"Why are you homeless? I always answer, by choice. Takes them awhile to come up with a followup.""And the second question?" Jake inquired.

"This place is run by a church, so they'll want to know if you need prayer."

"What do you say?"

"I always say, yes, but you need to come up with your own answer."

"Practice, do you need to pray with someone?" he asked, expecting him to rehearse.

Jake looked at him, puzzled.

"I'm fine."

"I don't think you'll get away with that answer."

"Why not?"

"Cause you're lying."

He stood up to leave.

"Wait a minute, where are you going?"

He turned to look at Jake sitting there like a helpless pup.

"Come with me."

They walked down a long hallway and into a room with four twin beds occupying the four corners.

"I sleep here, you can have that one over there," he said, pointing across the room.

"I'll show you where the facilities are cause man you need to shower."

"Okay."

Jake saw the bed had clean sheets, pillow, and a blanket folded at the end before leaving the room.

It felt good to stand under hot water, and Jake couldn't pull himself away. If only he could wash away the streak of bad luck, he thought. After the shower, he dressed in his dirty clothes catching his reflection in the mirror. His hair was longer and shaggy hanging over his ears and down the neckline, and he debated whether to shave thinking a beard would help disguise his appearance, and opted to go unshaven.

Chapter 36

Jake laid on the bed staring at the ceiling, having a difficult time accepting he was in a homeless shelter.

"You'd think after working fourteen hours, I could get some sleep," Al said.

Jake was confused.

"You have a job, but I saw you on the street."

"I'm homeless, not jobless. I stand there for a couple hours each evening to pick up extra cash before coming here," Al explained.

"Where do you work?"

"On a farm."

"Really."

"It's a pig farm, nothing glamorous, but it pays."

"I used to work on a farm."

"You don't look it."

"That's because I gave it up."

"For all of this," Jake said under his breath.

"There may be some work on the farm if you decide to get back into it."

"No way, I'm done with farm life."

"It's the Dickinson Farm, north on seventeen, if you change your mind."

"Thanks, but I'm good."

Jake stayed awake thinking about his life. One unfortunate mishap, and his world spiraled out of control. He couldn't help but think of Laura, reminiscing of their time together, and it hurt to learn that she was only interested in his money. In the back of his mind, he understood that he had only fallen for her charismatic personality. She was a good actress and nothing more.

He thought of Summer, and how she always had a concern for his wellbeing. Even though he didn't care for her forwardness, his best interest was her objective. She was a good person making a life for herself and doing it all alone. He respected that and believed she would be successful. He wanted to see her again, but that wasn't possible under these circumstances. Jake pulled the watch from his pocket, and held it in the darkened room. Memories rushed through him of his father, and he wondered how the business was doing. He replaced it and rolled onto his side, not accepting this was permanent.

Jake awoke to see that Al was gone. He went into the dining room, and ate breakfast before leaving the building. No one seemed to monitor the people coming and going. He roamed the streets without direction, and each evening, he went back to the shelter meeting Al at dinner.

"What are you planning to do with your life?" Al asked him.

"I don't know."

"It doesn't take long for the days to turn into months when you have food and shelter, and no one is making any demands."

"What are you saying?"

"You're a young man with your life ahead of you. With that college education, you don't belong in a homeless shelter. Make some quick cash, clean yourself up, and get a job. Earn a paycheck, save up, and start over."

Jake listened.

"There is still work on the pig farm, maybe you should try it."

That was a repulsive thought to Jake.

"I'll think about it."

Jake spent each day identical to the previous one, nothing was changing for him. After nearly three months, he knew Al was right, and life moves in one direction whether you are an active participant, or not. He spent an entire day sitting on a bench, and by nightfall decided to go the farm, and huddled next to a small shed for the night. He was jarred awake by the sound of a snorting pig.

Al saw him, and walked up with a newspaper folded under his arm and a Styrofoam cup of coffee. Apparently, he had just arrived to put in a days work.

"Didn't see you at the shelter last night," Al said.

"Yeah, I wasn't in the area."

"Did you come to work? There's plenty."

"I guess so."

"Good."

Jake noticed a picture on the front of the newspaper that Al had.

"Can I see that newspaper for a second?"

"Sure," Al said, handing it to him.

The headline read, "Notorious Mobster Arrested" with a picture of Frank. Jake quickly reads the brief article. "Frank D'Maggio was arrested yesterday at his restaurant in downtown Springfield after months of undercover surveillance exposed his embezzlement and money laundering, no bond will be set."

Jake was shocked to learn of Frank's extra-circular business activities realizing Laura's involvement also. He folded the newspaper, and handed it back to Al feeling relief that Frank was no longer a threat.

"Ready to do some work?"

"Okay."

Jake put in a fourteen hour day, exhausted when he returned to the shelter. He smelled of pig slop and sweat. After cleaning up, he met Al in the dining room.

"How did you like your first day?"

"It stunk," he replied.

"What? The pigs, or you?"

Jake grinned.

"Wow, that's the first time I've seen you smile."

"I haven't had anything to smile about."

He went with Al to the farm each day, and at the end of the week earned enough money to buy some clothes.

"Any inexpensive clothing stores around here?"

"On our pay, it can only be Goodwill, I'll take you in the morning."

"Thanks."

Jake bought one pair of jeans and two shirts, glad to have something clean to wear. He continued to work on the farm with Al, not seeing a future for himself yet. After nearly three months, they had developed a friendship, and Jake was comfortable in sharing his life.

"It's hard to believe that not long ago my life was so different."

"I imagine it was."

"Money is a powerful force," Jake told him, reminiscing.

"I wouldn't know."

"The fall from the top is a lot shorter than you might think, but no one ever tells you that," Jake confessed.

They were leaving the farm after putting in another day's work.

"Jake, it's real simple."

"What is?"

"You have a home, go back to it."

"No, I can't go back to the farm."

"Why not?"

"Because they wouldn't take me."

"They're your family."

"No, you don't understand. I abandoned them, and betrayed them. I can never go back."

Al studied Jake closely. He had taken him under his wing, but it was time to send him on his way; however, he realized Jake needed encouragement.

"You have a choice. You can stay here with the pigs, or go home to people who love you."

"How do you know they love me?"

"You've told me your father is a man of faith. If that's true, then he understands a love that is greater than all sin."

Jake pondered for a moment.

"I have a friend who predicted this," he said, remembering Summer.

"What's that?"

"That I would come face to face with myself. I don't know, I don't think I can face them."

Jake contemplated Al's words.

"Maybe I could earn their love by working on the farm just for food."

"Whatever will get you out of this pigpen," Al told him with a smile, patting him on the back.

"I don't believe for a minute that your father would expect you to work for food."

"Why not?"

"Because you're his son."

Jake wanted to go home, and make amends with his father. Al's words gave him courage.

"This is going to be more painful compared to losing all my stuff, I can tell you that."

"It might be easier than you think. Everything will be all right, you'll see. Your father must be a good man because he didn't hold you back from pursuing your dreams, and he'll equally embrace you when you return."

"Thanks, Al."

"Sure thing, kid."

After spending nearly six months living as a homeless person, Jake left the shelter the next morning wearing his new Goodwill clothes. He said goodbye to Al, and they parted walking in different directions. Jake was going home.

Chapter 37

Jake walked to a major highway, and thumbed his way north. He met various people along the way and many were truckers who paid for his meal at truck stops knowing he was broke, and traveling home. Jake figured they felt sorry for him. It took four days to get close enough to Calmar whereby he could walk the remaining distance. He had not bathed, and knew he looked as grungy as he felt.

He expected to see disappointment in his father's eyes, and Seth to ridicule him about everything, but he had no intention of countering whatever they had to say, he was defenseless. Jake knew enough to accept whatever verbal punishment his father and Seth administered. It couldn't be any worse than losing his inheritance, living in a shelter, and working on a pig farm.

It was midday when he came to the road that took him onto the private drive of the Abraham property. He stopped for a moment, taking a deep breath before walking down the lane with it's white fencing on either side. As he neared the house, he paused again, and looked around. He was home. It brought tears to his eyes, and he walked faster.

William and Seth were in the office with Seth speaking to Mrs. Grey while William looked out the front door. A figure caught his attention from a distance, and he wondered who would be walking on his property. As the man came closer, he recognized his son, and ran out the door.

"Dad," Seth called after him, not knowing what made him rush out of the office.

William sprinted all the way to his son. When Jake saw his father running towards him, he pick up his pace, and broke down crying and met in an embrace.

"I messed up, Dad. I lost it, I lost everything," Jake said, blurting out his failure as he sobbed on his father's shoulder.

"No Jake, you didn't lose us, you didn't lose me," his father told him, still holding tightly.

"You are my son, and you'll always be."

William released Jake and held his wet face in his hands, and drew him close pressing his forehead against Jake's.

"I am so glad you're home," he told him, and kissed his forehead.

"I love you, Jake. I'm thankful you came back."

"Me too."

Jake looked at his father through tear-filled eyes, and hugged him again.

"You never gave up on me, did you, Dad?"

"Never."

"I'm glad you didn't."

William held Jake tightly with his arm around his shoulder, and they walked down the lane.

"What's going on? I read an article that the farm was in trouble."

"Our Father provided, and all our prayers were answered."

William held his son close.

"All our prayers."

When they were close to the house, William yelled for everyone to gather around. Mrs. Grey ran out of the office up to Jake, and hugged him while men from the barn greeted him. Seth stood on the porch, and witnessed the scene before going inside. William put his arm around Jake's shoulder again, and they walked to the front door.

"I need to clean up," Jake said, entering through the office.

"Sure, son."

Jake went to his bedroom and took a long hot shower, putting on the robe that was still hanging on the back of his bathroom door. He noticed new clothes in his closet. His father called from the bedroom door and walked in.

"Jake, I have something for you."

William was holding a new pair of shoes, and handed them to him.

"When did you get these?"

"I bought them before you left."

He looked at the closet.

"Where did these clothes come from?"

"The clothes I bought for you, just in case."

Jake saw that his father expected him to return home, for the evidence was all around him. He never gave up on him, and Jake was humbled.

"One more thing, son. There's a ring I want you to have," William told him, handing Jake a signet ring that belonged to his great-great grandfather.

Jake accepted the ring, and saw that it was unique, and probably valuable.

"Who's ring is this?"

"It's been in our family for generations, and I want you to have it."

"Dad, I don't deserve any of this, it should go to Seth."

"You don't have to do anything to deserve it. I love you, son, always. I want you to understand that," William said, before leaving the room.

Jake sat on the edge of the bed unable to believe the unexpected reception from his father. He never knew how much his father loved him until this moment, nor how much he needed his father's love and acceptance. He wasn't worthy of anything, but was grateful just to be home. Jake remained in his room the rest of the afternoon, not wanting to interfere in the family.

Seth found his father in the living room, and sat on the edge of the opposite sofa. He'd overheard Mrs. Grey talking on the telephone about a party for Jake.

"You are throwing him a party," Seth said, indignant.

"Your brother has returned home."

"All these years I have worked with you, followed your guidance, and have done everything you asked of me. You never celebrated me like that."

"Seth, I've withheld nothing from you, everything I have is yours."

Seth stared at his father, angry. "Jake comes crawling back here after wasting everything on who knows what, and you want to celebrate that."

William hesitated before speaking. He wanted Seth to understand he wasn't showing favoritism.

"We're all together again, and we are celebrating your brother's return home because he was lost and now he's found."

William saw the turmoil in Seth and placed his hand on Seth's wanting him to accept his brother's return. Seth paused, dropping his head for a moment before looking at his father. He put his left hand on top of his father's and nodded in understanding. It wasn't his intent to upset him seeing his joy in having Jake home, so he withdrew his argument, but it was difficult for him to see Jake garnering all the attention.

Jake made an appearance at the dinner table. Seth and their father were already seated.

"Jake, there's a plate on the counter. I've already heated it up," his father told him.

"Thanks."

He took the plate, flatware, and went to sit in his usual chair, and it felt awkward.

"I see Dorothy is still cooking. I recognize this casserole dish," Jake said, trying to make conversation.

"I don't know what we would do without her," William said.

Jake glanced at Seth who had yet to say a word to him since he arrived. He could only imagine what was going through his mind, and waited for Seth to speak. This time, he would keep his peace.

"Jake, I want to throw a party and invite all our friends, and let everyone know you have come home."

Jake looked at Seth.

"Dad, that's not necessary."

"I know, but I want to. I'm so glad to have you with us again."

"It's good to be home," Jake admitted.

"I've had plenty of time to think before coming back, and I wasn't certain you wanted me here."

"That isn't true."

Again, Jake looked at Seth who remained silent.

"I'll work on the farm in whatever job you give me. If it's in the fields, I'll do it."

"That would be a first," Seth said, finally speaking.

Jake ignored Seth's comment.

"What I'm saying is I don't deserve anything from the family, but I'm grateful to be welcomed back."

"That's a matter of opinion," Seth said.

Jake didn't say anymore and ate his meal, listening to Seth and their father discussing issues on the farm. He'd been out of the loop for some time, and even though these were not new concerns from Jake's prospective, he didn't offer any input.

Jake excused himself to sit in the living room. His father joined him thirty minutes later. He needed to talk with his father, and with Seth before too many days passed because it was important to make amends with them.

William sat down on the sofa opposite Jake.

"I'm blessed to have you home. I prayed everyday for your safety, and that perhaps you would contact me, and tell me you were alright."

He hesitated before speaking again.

"I called you once right after you left. When you didn't answer, I knew you were breaking all ties."

"I was determined to get away, and so sure there was a better life, I wanted to be a part of it."

Jake paused.

"I learned that one day you can be on top, and one mishap can bring you down," he said, remembering.

William just listened.

"I left here determined to live the rich life, and I succeeded for a short time. I bought a condo in the city, a Maserati, ate at the finest restaurants, and for a while life was just the way I imagined."

"What happened?"

"Bad investment with the wrong people, and lost everything. I became homeless virtually overnight, resorted to living on the street by day, and a homeless shelter at night."

"Why didn't you come home?"

"At first, I was ashamed and didn't want to face you, but as time passed, I didn't think you would want me back."

"How could you ever think that, son?"

"I'd be an embarrassment to you."

"Never."

"Truthfully, I'm not sure I would've returned if not for a man I met at the shelter."

"Then I owe this man a debt of gratitude," William said.

"I meant what I said earlier. I will put in a full days work, and do whatever you want me to do."

William watched his son.

"First thing in the morning, let's get you set up in your office, and Mrs. Grey can bring you up-to-date on the business."

Jake is shocked.

"Dad, I don't deserve to have everything as it was."

"I am not having you waste your college education working in the fields."

Jake smiled at his father.

"Thanks, Dad."

"No son, thank you for coming home."

Jake embraced his father, and left him sitting alone. William thanked God for answering his prayers, and took his Bible to read.

Chapter 38

Jake went into the kitchen to get a drink of water, and stood at the kitchen sink looking out the window over the back lawn. He turned when Seth walked in, but didn't say anything, waiting for Seth to speak.

"You should have stayed away," Seth told him.

"Probably."

"Why did you come back?"

"I had no where to go."

"Bet you blew your inheritance."

"That's true."

"Think you can just pick up where you left off."

"No, Seth. I can't do that."

"I give you one day, and you'll up to your old tricks again."

Jake hesitated before speaking.

"I don't have any tricks, I don't have any money, I don't have anything. I came home because my choices were to live in a homeless shelter, or come home and start over. There is one thing I have learned, and that is to not take anything for granted."

Seth was about to make a comment, but Jake threw up his hand to forestall him. Jake figured it was as good a time as any to speak his mind.

"I have no intentions of leaving again. I will do my share of the work and responsibilities on the farm."

Seth didn't know how to respond. This wasn't the carefree and irresponsible Jake who left home a year ago, he had matured.

"It's your decision, Seth, how we work together."

William had been standing in the doorway and heard the conversation. Jake walked out of the kitchen passing him, unconcerned that he overheard. Seth turned to see his father.

"You heard?"

"I did. Jake is reaching out to you as a brother."

William left in search of Jake, finding him outside on the porch, and stood beside his son in silence for a moment.

"You've changed."

"I've grown up."

"You've become a man who knows himself, it's a good place to be."

"Something I learned in that big world out there," he said, looking out over the land.

"About that party, Dad. When did you plan to have it?"

"I thought maybe in a week. That would give Mrs. Grey enough time to spread the word."

"There is someone I want you to meet, but I have to go back to the city. I'd be gone a couple of days," Jake said.

"You don't need my permission."

"You've never asked me where I've been."

"You'd tell me, if I needed to know."

Jake looked at his father.

"I was in Missouri, Springfield to be exact."

William nodded.

"Can I borrow the SUV on Thursday? If I leave early, I should make it in a day and be back Friday night."

"That's fine, son. We'll have the party on Saturday afternoon."

"Thanks," Jake said.

The next morning, Jake was up early and waiting for Mrs Grey when she came in.

"Jake, this is a surprise."

William walked into the office at the same time.

"Jake will be back in his office, so we need to get it in order, and go over the accounts with him."

"Sure thing."

"What do you want to do first, Jake?"

"I'm not sure."

"Why don't we start with the office? We can clean out some things that don't belong."

"Sounds good."

They went into his office that now looked more like a storage room.

"What happened here?"

"It became a catchall for anything we didn't have a home for," she told him.

They sorted through stacks of papers, magazines, books, and files. Jake turned on the computer, and noticed all the programs were still there. He spent the next two days reacquainting himself with the business.

Early Thursday morning, he left for Springfield, hoping it was a successful trip.

Chapter 39

Knowing his destination, Jake only stopped for gas and a sandwich at a convenience store, and pulled into a roadside motel with no intention of returning to the Lincoln Plaza Hotel. Along with borrowing the company SUV, his father gave him a credit card to cover his expenses. The next morning, he was at Strutton and Associates when they opened.

"Mr. Abraham, I'm surprised to see you," Sandra said, when he walked into her office.

"I wasn't at my best the last time I was here," he said as an apology.

"I came to ask you to put my condominium on the market."

"I'm sorry, but the condo doesn't belong to you. When you didn't make the monthly payments, the property reverted to the original owner, and they now have possession. It was in the fine print of your contract."

"I didn't realize that. I was hoping to recoup some of the money I invested in it."

"If you will leave an address and phone number where I can reach you, I'll be glad to speak with them, and see if they will consider a partial reimbursement of your down payment since you didn't occupy the unit for very long."

Jake hesitated, but decided to give Sandra the information.

"I want it kept confidential. It cannot be given out under any circumstance."

"I understand."

Sandra believed she knew who he didn't want having his address.

"I assume you've read the paper about Frank?"

"Yes."

"That was quite a shock. Laura wasted no time in leaving town. Probably didn't want to be connected with Frank when he goes to trial," Sandra told him.

Jake didn't care what happened to Frank, or Laura. When he didn't respond, Sandra dropped the subject.

"I wish you well, Mr. Abraham," she said, reaching across her desk to shake his hand.

"Same to you, and thank you."

Everything pertaining to his life in the city was gone, so he shouldn't be surprised when the condo was no longer an option, he thought. His next stop was Siesta to see Summer, for she was his reason for returning to Springfield.

She was working behind the counter with her back to the door and when she turned, he was standing at the counter.

"Jake," she said, stunned to see him.

Summer almost dropped a cup she was holding.

"It's me."

"I didn't think I'd ever see you again."

"I wasn't so sure myself."

"You look much better then the last time I saw you," she told him.

"I hope so."

"You seem content. What's happened?"

"I went home."

"I'm glad. Is your family's business doing alright?"

"Yes, it's okay."

"Did you want something to drink? A Raspberry Mocha, perhaps."

"No, maybe an Expresso Romano."

"Coming right up, Mr. Trump."

"Just call me Jake, all my friends do."

"Of course."

They laughed.

"If you went home, then what are you doing in the city?"

"I came to see you."

"Me?"

"Can you take a break, I need to talk to you."

"Sure, I'll get someone to cover for me."

Summer went to the back, and returned with a young girl following her.

"I'm taking an early lunch break. Do you want to go to the deli?"

"Okay."

They took a seat away from the other customers. Are you hungry?" Jake asked.

"No, I'm fine."

"When did you go home?" she asked, curious.

"A few days ago."

"Where have you been all this time?"

Jake was embarrassed to tell her, but wasn't going to lie.

"I roamed the streets, slept in a homeless shelter, and worked on a pig farm."

"Oh my goodness. I'm so sorry to hear that."

"Why didn't you go home when you lost your money?"

"I was ashamed, and I didn't think my family wanted me."

"How can you say that?"

"That's exactly what my father said."

"He's your father, he loves you. It doesn't make sense to not go back to the people who care."

"Do you care, Summer, or have I destroyed the feelings I know you had for me?"

She wasn't sure how much she was willing to reveal, guarding her heart.

"I care. I'm happy to see you're safe with your family, and that you're doing well."

"Will you forgive my bad behavior?"

She could see his sincerity.

"You're already forgiven."

"I want to start over with you, if you'll give me the chance to prove I'm not the same person you first met."

"I never believed that was the real you."

"How's that?"

"I saw a man with a good heart, but I also knew you were lost and hurting. I saw it in you because there was a time when the same feelings were in me, searching to find myself, and where I belonged in this world. You and I both came to the city for a new beginning, something we had in common. Maybe that is what drew me to you, and my desire to help you."

Jake listened without interrupting.

"I've had plenty of time to think since our last conversation, and truthfully, I didn't expect to see you again, though I prayed for your wellbeing," she continued.

"I went home expecting the worst, but my father didn't ridicule me for squandering my inheritance, but welcomed me home."

"Of course, you're his son, and he'll always love you."

"I didn't understand that until now."

"I'm glad you do."

"Summer, will you give me another chance? I can be the person you believed in."

"I see that."

She watched him carefully, and knew this was the real Jacob Abraham.

"Yes, Jake, I want that too."

He reached across the table, and took her hands in his.

"Thank you."

"For what?"

"For believing in me, forgiving me, and giving me a second chance."

She smiled at him.

"My father is throwing a party tomorrow afternoon at the farm. Will you come with me, and meet my family?"

Summer was quite surprised, not expecting to meet his family.

"I have to work."

"Do you want to come with me?"

She wanted to spend time with Jake, and had always wanted time with him when he was living in the city.

"Yes, but I need to get someone to cover my shift for the weekend. If the party is tomorrow, how will we get there in time?"

"I have to leave soon. I know I'm springing this on you without giving you a chance to think about it and prepare," he told her.

"It is quick."

She didn't have class on Friday night, and knew she could get help at the cafe. Something within her was compelling her to not let this opportunity slip away for her sake and Jake's. For a fleeting moment, Mr. Foster's words echoed in her head, that if it's meant to be, it will be, for God would see to it. It felt right.

Chapter 40

Summer quickly packed an overnight bag, while Jake waited in her small apartment. He looked around, everything reflected her personality, and noticed she liked various shades of pink. He saw a picture of an older couple guessing them to be her parents, and another of a young woman holding a baby, probably her sister.

A tall bookshelf was overloaded with books, and a coffee table covered with papers and schoolbooks which reminded him of his dorm room when he was in college. She came out of the bedroom with her bag, and Jake placed it in the SUV.

"Unless we drive through the night, we'll need to stop overnight. Are you okay with that? I'll get two rooms, you'll be safe with me," he said, winking at her.

She laughed.

"Jake, if I didn't think I'd be safe with you, I never would have agreed to this trip."

"Right."

The drive was enjoyable as they chatted about various topics. She told him of her intent next semester to double her classes, so she could graduate in a year, eager to move forward with her life. Jake shared bits of information about the farm and his father. They didn't have anything to eat before leaving the city, and stopped after a few hours for an early dinner.

Summer was happy to be with Jake. He was proving to be the man she always believed him to be. They stopped after dark, and Jake paid for two rooms at a Marriott just off the main highway. They agreed to meet in the lobby for the continental breakfast at six in the morning, and were back on the road by seven.

Jake phoned his father, expecting to arrive by noon, and William informed him that was the time the party began. Jake planned to be on time, after all, the party was in his honor. As they neared Calmar, Summer focused on the openness of the country, so different from the city.

When they pulled off the main highway onto a less congested road, Jake drove slower before stopping at the entrance to the Abraham farm with a large sign to the right announcing the property. Summer's eyes grew big, for she had never seen anything like it. Even from the road, she saw it was a big operation, and turned to look at Jake.

"I didn't know your farm was so large."

"One of a handful in the state this size."

"I always thought it was a small, family farm."

"It is, except it isn't small."

"I see that," she said, staring out the window.

"Are you ready to meet my family?"

"I'm not sure."

"Don't get cold feet on me," he said, teasing her.

She took a deep breath.

"Okay, I'm ready."

He looked at her and grinned.

Slowly driving down the lane, Summer was fascinated with the white picket fence and the landscape. She could see the house, and a large gathering of people off to the side near a huge barn. Jake parked in front of the house, and Summer stood at the opened SUV door with Jake watching her amazed expression.

"Come on, it's fine," he said, taking her hand.

William saw them drive up, and walked towards them. He didn't realize the person Jake wanted him to meet was a woman. As he drew closer, William was surprised for a moment.

"Dad, this is Summer Marie Fellows," he said, speaking first.

Summer smiled at Jake for saying her full name.

"This is my father, William Abraham."

"Mr. Abraham, it's a pleasure to meet you," she said, extending her hand.

William took her hand in his, but didn't shake it. Instead, he held it and placed his other hand on top of hers.

"It's good to meet you, Summer."

"Son," William said, patting him on the back.

"Got the grills fired up, so let's go join the party."

"Great," Jake replied, excited.

They walked towards the crowd, and people began rushing up to them. All of a sudden they were surrounded, and Jake couldn't keep up with the introductions. Summer was awed as she stood by his side, and William stepped away from the limelight to observe his son.

He couldn't take his eyes off of Summer. She was young and pretty with a fondness for Jake that was obvious. William felt as though he had stepped inside a time machine and gone back forty years. She was Marybeth with the same features and coloring and the more he watched her, he noted that even her mannerisms were similar. Summer even threw her head back the same way Marybeth did when she laughed. He wondered if Jake saw the resemblance.

Mrs. Grey wasted no time in meeting Jake's young woman, taking an instant liking to her. Summer reminded her of someone, but she couldn't place the face. It would come to her later, she thought. She fixed them plates of hamburgers, potato salad, beans, and glasses of iced tea. As they stood around eating, Jake was continuously approached by the employees and friends of the family, welcoming him home.

Jake was humbled by the reception of so many people, understanding that he was a member of the team that made up the Abraham Organic Farm, and never considered how much he was loved by his father, and respected by the employees. He was so glad to be home, and given a new beginning in his life. Things would be different.

Seth stood at the entrance to the barn, and watched the scene. He didn't agree with the party, and had no intention of being a part of the welcoming committee. He contemplated the last conversation with Jake, and knew that whatever his brother had experienced, it made him a different person.

Seth walked into the crowd towards a table of food. Jake noticed Seth and walked up to him.

"Thanks Seth, for coming to my party," he said, sincerely.

"I came to get something to eat."

Jake ignored his comment.

"Doesn't matter; you're here. It's important to me."

Seth didn't know what to say and continued fixing a plate. Jake put his hand on Seth's shoulder and squeezed before leaving his side. Seth watched him walk over to his girlfriend who was standing with Mrs. Grey. He took his plate to stand off to the side, not knowing how to respond to Jake's affectionate gesture.

William watched from the edge of the crowd and though he didn't hear the conversation, he could see Jake's attempts to show Seth he loved him, and wanted them to be brothers in heart as well as in blood. He smiled a silent prayer of thanksgiving, for he was able to see his sons together again.

The party dispersed near dusk with the men returning the grills to the barn, while Mrs. Grey and Summer put the food inside the house. William walked up to Jake, standing alone.

"It was a good party," Jake told him.

"We had something to celebrate."

"It was a hard lesson, but I learned it well. It took hitting bottom for me to understand the love that was always here even when I didn't feel it, or believe it; your love, Dad."

"I'm glad you know that."

"I haven't forgotten your ideas for the business and the first opportunity we have, I'm calling a meeting of everyone involved, and we're going to sit down and talk about implementing some of those suggestions. If it helps us to run a more efficient business, and save money in the process, I'm for that."

Jake was shocked to hear his father say that.

"I thought you didn't agree with my ideas."

"I agreed, it was the timing that I questioned."

"And you feel the time is now right."

"Yes, it's time to make some changes."

Jake grinned.

"Cool," he said, making his father laugh.

They walked together inside the house to find the women in the kitchen wrapping food, and storing it in the refrigerator.

"You've got enough food for a week," Mrs. Grey told him.

"Good, Dorothy won't need to cook," William replied.

Jake watched Summer helping Mrs. Grey. He walked up to her at the counter.

"Are you having fun?"

"I am."

Mrs. Grey noticed William watching them, and smiled.

"Well, I'll be on my way. Summer it's a pleasure to meet you, and I hop to see you again.

"Thank you."

"I'll walk you to the door," William said.

While driving home, Mrs. Grey remembered why Summer looked so familiar to her. It was from the pictures around the house of Mr. Abraham's wife, Marybeth. That's where she had seen her face. What an amazing resemblance, she thought.

Chapter 41

William, Jake, and Summer went to sit in the living room. Jake and Summer sat close together on the sofa while William took a chair across from them. He tried not to stare, but couldn't stop reminiscing of his own life when he was that age with his sweetheart.

"You have a lovely home, Mr. Abraham," Summer spoke first.

"Thank you. I grew up in this house, and when I married, my wife and I raised our boys here," he told her.

"It must be wonderful to have a special home with all the memories."

"It is."

William was curious how they met, but wasn't going to ask questions. Summer talked about her parent's death, moving to the city, and attending college. William understood her ambition, and saw that she had learned to make it on her own.

"It must have been hard for you. I can understand because my wife was in an accident, and my sons were left without a mother."

"Jake told me. I'm sorry for your loss."

"And yours," he said.

"Did Jake tell you how we met?" she asked, glancing at him.

"No, he hasn't."

"In a coffee shop where I work."

William found that interesting, recalling his first date with Marybeth was in a diner. Another similarity, he thought.

"He would come for an Expresso Romano," she said, teasingly.

"I really went to see you. Okay, it was for the coffee, and to see you," Jake said, laughing.

William saw it as a blessing to have Jake sitting here with his friend, relaxed, and in good spirits. It had been a long time since he heard the sound of laughter, and Summer's presence was refreshing, and much needed in their home, he realized. Seth entered the room, having not been officially introduced to Summer, and sat down in the chair opposite his father.

"This is my older brother, Seth, and this is Summer Fellows" Jake said, making the introductions.

Seth didn't know what to say to Summer. The only female they've had in the house was Mrs. Grey and Dorothy, so it was strange to have a woman sitting in their living room.

"Seth, it's nice to meet you," she said.

"Yeah, you too."

"How long will you be staying?" Seth asked, pointedly.

"I'm taking Summer home on Monday," Jake replied.

"So you won't be here next week."

Seth was referring to Jake.

"I should be back late Tuesday."

"What's the plan for tomorrow?" Seth asked.

"I'm showing Summer the farm, and maybe a drive into town."

"Did you have something in mind, Seth?" Jake asked.

"No. I've got things to do," Seth said, leaving the room, abruptly.

William watched the scene unfold. There was something about Summer that was affecting the Abraham men, including himself. They talked about the farm, and William spoke of Marybeth. Though he thought of her everyday, he wasn't accustomed to speaking openly about his wife, but it was comforting to do so with Summer, perhaps because of the similarities. He wondered if they'd had a girl, would she have looked like Summer.

William excused himself leaving them alone the remainder of the evening, taking his Bible to his bedroom to read. The house had a guest room, and Jake put her things in there. The next morning, after a breakfast of muffins and coffee, he drove her around the farm in the SUV.

"I'm really impressed," she told him.

"There's nothing impressive about corn."

"Sure there is, this is an amazing operation. I'm in awe of it, and you should be too."

"Why is that?"

"Because this is a legacy that's been passed down through generations, and one day it will belong to you and Seth, and then your children; it's truly magnificent. Don't you understand what you have here?"

"I never thought of it that way."

"Well, you should. You have something priceless in your family business, and you are a vital part of it."

Jake pondered her words. He never considered the farm as anything other then cornfields. To see it as a tradition, a legacy to be carried on to the next generation wasn't something he thought about, but maybe it was time he did.

He parked the SUV, and they walked through the barns, and he showed her the large equipment, and how it removed the corn from the husk. He explained in detail the many facets involved in the production process. Summer was learning about Jake's life and felt privileged to be with him. He was so different here than in the city.

William and Seth watched them entering the barn from the front porch. It was wonderful having Jake home, and an added blessing to see him with Summer, like reliving life with Marybeth through his son. He still didn't think Jake made the connection, and debated if he should say anything to him.

"It sure is good to have Jake home," William said.

"You would think that."

"I have both my sons, and I couldn't be more content."

"What do you make of Summer?" Seth asked.

"What do you mean?"

"Haven't you noticed the resemblance."

"So, you see it too."

"How could I not? In fact, it's spooky how much she looks like mom."

"I don't think Jake realizes it, though," William said.

There was silence between them for a moment.

"I didn't mean to be rude to her last night, but it was uncomfortable, made me feel like I was sitting across from mom."

"Maybe we should tell them," William said.

"Not me."

Jake and Summer walked towards them.

"You have a wonderful farm, Mr. Abraham," Summer said.

"Thank you."

"You must be very proud."

"I guess Jake has told you it's been in the family a long time."

"Yes, and a wonderful legacy to leave to your sons, and then their children, that's really awesome."

William saw how easy it was to be around Summer with her kind and compassionate nature, a gentle spirit. If Jake should marry, Summer would be a positive addition to their family, he thought. He could tell she cared for him and to bring her to the farm, he could only surmise it was mutual.

"I'll go fix dinner, and see you later," he said.

Seth felt strange standing with Jake and his girlfriend, not knowing what to say.

"I've got some work to do in the barn," he said, leaving them alone.

"Your brother doesn't have much to say."

"He might feel intimidated."

"I don't understand."

"Seth always has something to say, but around you, he's silent," Jake said, watching his brother walk away.

"I hope I'm not making your family feel uncomfortable, you know, a woman on the premises."

"No, that's not it, but even so, they'll have to get used to it because I want you to come to the farm more often."

They sat down on the steps of the porch.

"How do you feel about long distance relationships?" he asked.

"I don't know, I've never had one," she replied, grinning.

"Are you willing to have one with me?"

She looked at him.

"I would love that."

"Great. I'll come to the city as often as I can, and maybe you can come here when you get a chance. I can pick you up and take you back."

"That's a lot of driving."

"You're worth it."

"You're not the same Jake I first met."

"I'm not that person anymore. Falling from the top changed me, but for the better."

"Do you miss that lifestyle, and the money?"

"Not at all. You would think so, but I don't."

"Then you really have changed."

Jake reached for her hand entwining her fingers with his. That was how William found them when he stepped on the porch to announce dinner was ready. It put a smile on his face.

Chapter 42

They left early Monday morning before dawn with Summer having evening classes, and due back at work on Wednesday. The long drive back to Springfield was bittersweet for Summer. Over the weekend, they made a commitment to each other, and she knew it would be hard not seeing him for possibly weeks at a time.

Jake drove to her apartment, and waited for her to freshen up as she had to hurry to the university. He wanted to kiss her before leaving, but didn't want to be too forward in the early stage of their newfound relationship. Jake played it safe and asked.

"Do you mind if I kiss you before I leave?"

"I've been waiting for one, Mr. Abraham," she said with a smile.

He grinned at her formality.

Jake leaned in and kissed her, a sweet and gentle kiss.

"That was nice. May I have one more?" she asked, teasingly.

Jake kissed her again, and Summer put her arms around his neck. Neither wanted to separate, but it was necessary.

"I have to leave, so you can get to class on time."

"Will you call me later?"

"I'll call you everyday until we see each other again."

"Perfect."

Summer gathered her school books, and walked outside with Jake. He drove long into the night knowing he needed to get back, and be at work on Wednesday, accepting his presence on the farm would be different.

Jake had plenty of time to think while driving home, and thought often of Summer and her presence on the farm, something he never anticipated. He recalled their conversations, and how she saw the farm through unrestrained eyes, the real inheritance was in the legacy. She was unaware of the significance of her comments, but it helped him to understand his place and value as a son in the Abraham family, and his rightful heritage.

Jake finally understood that what he was searching for was something money couldn't buy, acceptance and love. It was a hard lesson to learn, but a valuable one, for the city life and money he coveted was a facade, and never could have provided him true happiness. In losing everything tangible, he gained much more, the true value of family, friends, love, and belonging. He had grown into the man he wanted to become.

The next morning, he checked out of a roadside hotel early, excited to be going home and ready to be an active participant in the family. Jake drove down the long winding lane, and stopped when he saw an employee and friend.

"Morning Jose, how are you?"

"Good morning, Mr. Abraham, it's good to have you back."

"Thanks, but lose the mister, save it for my father."

"If you say so."

"We're friends, no need. Want to have lunch later this week?" Jake asked.

"Alright."

"Good, I'll talk to you later."

"Sure thing."

Jake parked in front of the house, and walked through the office carrying his overnight bag.

"You're back early. We weren't expecting you until this evening," Mrs. Grey said.

"Got things to do."

"Good to have you home."

"Thanks, I'll be back in a few minutes."

"No hurry."

Jake went to his bedroom and unpacked, then into the kitchen and opened the refrigerator to look for something to eat. He saw Seth's sandwich but chose something from the freezer, and defrosted it. While he was waiting, his father came in.

"Jake, I didn't know you were back."

"Just got here a few minutes ago."

"How was the trip?"

"Long."

He carried his casserole to the table while William heated leftovers, and joined him. It felt like old times sitting at the table with his youngest.

"I read about the drought in the paper, but it looks like you've had rain."

"We finally did."

"I appreciated the party, it was good to see everyone again."

"I know you didn't believe me when I said you'd be missed. It wasn't just me, it was everyone who is connected with this farm, and our friends," William said.

"I understand that now."

"What do you want me to do on the farm, Dad?"

"I want you to apply your education and help make this business better for generations to follow."

Jake smiled at his father.

"That would be my children and Seth's."

"That's right, prepare the business for your children."

"I can do that."

"Don't forget to share your thoughts with the rest of us," William said with humor.

"I get it," Jake said, laughing.

Seth entered to the sound of their father and Jake laughing. He opened the refrigerator to see his sandwich was still there, and glanced to see what Jake was eating. He joined them at the table.

"What's so funny?"

"Talking about children," William said, eyeing Jake.

"Whose children?"

"Ours," Jake replied, without elaborating.

Seth looked confused, causing William and Jake to chuckled.

"Is someone going to let me in on the joke?" Seth asked, agitated.

"Dad and I were talking about preparing the business for the next generation," Jake explained.

Seth still looked dumbfounded.

"Yours and my children, big brother. The next generation of Abraham's."

That was a frightening thought to Seth, one he had never considered. After spending his days caring for the farm, there wasn't time to think about the generation that follows after them. Seth knew that he may not have any children to inherit his portion of the business. It could all go to Jake's children.

"You look pale. Are you feeling all right, Seth?" his father asked.

"I don't expect to have children," Seth announced.

"Why not?" William asked.

"Because he has to get off this farm long enough to meet a woman, and you should do just that Seth. I'll do your work while you take a break, and do some exploring of your own. You've spent your entire life dedicated to this business, and it's your turn to leave and do something else for a while," Jake said, answering his father's question.

Seth studied Jake. He didn't think his brother was pushing him off the farm, and out of the business because he could see the genuine sincerity in his eyes, and didn't know how to feel about Jake's directness.

"Give it some thought, Seth. You deserve it, and I know that. Show me your schedule, and allow me to do this for you."

William listened and couldn't have been more proud of Jacob, then he was at that moment. It was the most generous gift Jake could have given to his brother, a gift of love, but it would be up to Seth to receive it. Seth didn't know how to respond.

"I'll think about it," he replied, uneasy.

Seth couldn't think of anything to say to Jake, unsettled by his words, attitude, and a commitment to be brothers. Things just weren't the way they used to be since Jake came home.

Chapter 43

Jake spent the first week in the office. Mrs. Grey updated him on the business affairs. He chose to spend the second week working in the fields with the men.

"Mrs. Grey, can you spare me for a week?" Jake asked.

"What do you mean?"

"I'll be working outside this week."

"I did it while you were gone, so I'm sure another week won't make a difference," she replied with humor.

"Thanks. Anything comes up, you'll know where to find me."

Mrs. Grey was pleased to see the change in Jake.

Monday morning, he was driving the tractor out in the fields before Seth made it to the barn. The men were pleased to see him, and treated Jake with respect and friendship. He worked taking soil samples for nutrient density, checking for pestilence, and surveying the land. At the end of each day, he walked through the office dirty, exhausted, and happy. Jake took pride in the knowledge that the Abraham farm belonged to him in partnership with his brother.

William came out of his office to see Jake walking through the house. He glanced at Mrs. Grey and smiled.

"Jake is a new man," she told him.

"I couldn't agree more."

"Whatever he experienced had a major impact."

"I'm just thankful he's home," William told her.

"Me too."

After cleaning up, Jake went into the kitchen to take out one of Dorothy's homemade dinners. Seth came in from the barn for a drink of water. Neither spoke as Jake was waiting to see what Seth had to say to him.

"You've never worked in the fields, so why now? What are you trying to prove?" Seth asked, sternly.

The bell on the microwave signaled his food was ready, and Jake carried it to the table followed by Seth with his glass of water.

"I don't believe you've changed one bit. I think you're the same old Jake, but you want to win the good graces of everyone, so you're playing the good guy routine, you don't fool me."

Jake ate his food unperturbed by Seth's comment.

"I have changed whether you accept it, or not. I wasn't a very considerate person, but I've learned to become one."

Jake finished his meal, taking his plate to the sink, and left Seth sitting alone.

The third week, Jake worked in the barn with the large machinery processing the corn into bins. Though the massive machines did the work, he stood alongside the men moving large bins of corn, sealing the lids, and stacking them with a forklift in a separate area for pickup.

William was amazed to see the contribution Jake was making on the farm. Approximately three weeks after Jake's return home, Sid visited.

"Mr. Rothenberg, good to see you again," Mrs. Grey said, looking up from her work.

"How are you doing, Mrs. Grey?"

"Couldn't be better," she said, smiling.

"I took a chance in driving out, hoping to see Abe."

"In his office, just tap on the door."

"Thanks."

Sid knocked before entering, and they shook hands.

"I won't take much time, but since I didn't make it to Jake's homecoming party, thought I'd come out to see him."

"Glad you did."

"Everything worked out for him and for you, my friend. Prayers were answered, God always comes through."

"He does."

"Is Jake in his office?"

"He's in the barn, let's take a walk out there," William said.

They went to the barn stopping at the entrance, and observed the production. Spotting Jake with his arms in corn up to his elbows, they watched him for a moment. He looked content, conversing with the man standing beside him.

"Now, that's a good sight," Sid said.

"It is."

Jake saw his father and Sid watching from the doorway, and walked over to them.

"Hey, Sid, good to see you. I'd shake your hand, but as you can see, mine are dirty."

Sid patted Jake on the shoulder.

"Great to see you, Jake. Has life been treating you right?"

"It is now," he replied with a grin.

"I stopped by to see you, since I didn't make it for your party."

"I appreciate that. I should get back to work, but I'm sure I'll see you again soon."

"That you will."

Jake returned to the machinery while William and Sid watched.

"I don't see Seth?"

"Probably in the field."

"How's he handling Jake being home?"

"That's an interesting thing. Jake has changed, and Seth is having to respond differently to his brother. How can you argue with someone who uses kindness as their arsenal?"

"Got a point," Sid told him.

They left the barn, and William walked him to his car.

"I appreciate you coming by today."

Sid nodded.

William watched him drive down the lane before returning to his office. Seth was nowhere in sight.

Chapter 44

Jake had been home three months and was working in his office studying software programs and putting together analysis of several companies to determine which programs would be best suited for their business. It was a time consuming task, but he wanted to have a proposal to present to the team.

One of the first changes made to the business was having monthly meetings of the key people with each expressing their ideas and concerns in their given arena. The team consisted of William, Seth, Jake, Mrs. Grey, and Samuel. Jake's motto of "work smarter not harder" became the theme. Jake was responsible for conducting their meetings, and everyone liked the idea including Seth.

They shared ideas of streamlining production through Samuel's input, to programs that would help Mrs. Grey perform her duties more efficiently. No new program was implemented without a vote from the team and a plan. William sat during these occasions and listened knowing the business would thrive. Both his boys expressed a love of the family business, and between the two of them it would prosper, and be ready for the next generation.

Mrs. Grey interrupted Jake's work with a letter that arrived.

"Jake, sorry to bother you, but this came in the mail today," she said, handing it to him.

Jake turned around in his chair.

"Thanks."

He looked at the return address on the envelope and recognized the name, Strutton and Associates. When he opened it, a check fell to the floor, and he picked it up to see the amount, and was shocked that it was for two hundred thousand dollars. He read the accompanying letter from Sandra, stating that the condominium was under a new lease-to-purchase agreement, and because this occurred relatively quick, the owners were compelled to return a significant portion of his deposit. Jake focused on the check, and reread the letter.

He placed the check and letter inside the envelope, and put it in his desk drawer. He had been given nearly a quarter of his inheritance. Surprisingly, his first reaction wasn't to reinvest, though he believed himself good at the skill, it didn't hold the same appeal. He turned back to the computer and decided to not mention the money, needing to think about it.

William was thankful to experience evening meals with enjoyment, and conversations were interesting.

"How's Summer doing in school?" he asked.

"Good, she talked with her counselor, and by adding a few classes to each semester, she'll move her graduation to next year."

"That's great. She's a smart girl, and handling her life maturely," William replied.

"She is the most positive, upbeat person I have ever known, and we talk daily."

"When will she be coming back to visit?"

"She's studying for finals, so may be a few more weeks."

"I look forward it."

"I can't wait to see her, either."

Seth ate his dinner in silence listening to them talk. A week after receiving the check, Jake knew what he wanted to do with the money. He took the check out of the envelope, and placed it on top of the dresser in his bedroom. After dinner that evening, he found Seth alone in the living room. Jake returned to his room for the check, and went back to sit in the chair opposite Seth. Jake waited for Seth's attention, and handed him the check.

"What's this?" Seth asked, looking at the amount.

"The owners of the condominium I bought in the city were kind enough to return some of my deposit."

"So why are you showing this to me?" Seth asked, confused.

"I'm not showing it to you, I'm giving it to you."

Seth was even more astounded.

"I don't get it."

"I understand you took money from your portfolio to support the farm during the drought, and I want you to have this as a payback."

"How did you find out about that?"

"It slipped when Mrs. Grey was going over the business. I don't think she realized what she said. It doesn't matter that I know, I would've given it to you anyway. I don't need it."

Seth was speechless.

"Thank you for taking care of the family business, and watching out for dad in my absence. This isn't much, but I want you to have it," Jake told him, before leaving the room.

Seth looked at the check again, totally shocked. William passed Jake in the hallway before walking into the living room. He sat down and took his Bible off the table, but before opening it, looked at Seth.

"What's wrong, Seth?"

William noticed him holding a piece of paper, but didn't inquire what it was. Seth leaned forward, and handed it to his father. William saw it was a check, and looked at the amount and then back a Seth. It was payable to Jacob Abraham.

"Who's Strutton and Associates? What is this?" William asked.

"It's the deposit Jake made on a condominium. Apparently they resold it, and returned his money."

"Why do you have it?"

"He gave it to me, said he didn't need it."

William understood the lessons Jake learned ran deep. He knew his son could have kept the money and never mentioned it, reinvested to attempt to make more, or a dozen other things, but instead he gave it away.

"What will you do with it?"

Seth thought for a moment.

"Take half and replace the money taken from my IRA, and the other half create a new portfolio for Jake," Seth said.

"Are you sure?"

"Yes."

"I'll call Cliff in the morning."

William paused before speaking again.

"You know, Seth, this was a generous gift Jake has given you, it's much deeper then money."

"I get that, Dad."

"I figured you did."

William took his Bible and went to his bedroom to read, putting the check on the nightstand to handle in the morning. Seth remained in the living room, and thought about everything that had transpired since Jake returned home.

The next morning, William went to Jake's office and stood in the doorway, watching him for a few seconds before speaking.

"Is that a new program?" his father asked.

Jake kept working on the computer, punching keys on the keypad.

"I'm checking out a new accounting software. It appears to be designed with manufacturing and production platforms."

"Do you find it acceptable?" William asked.

"Looks promising."

William waited until Jake gave him his undivided attention. Jake turned around, and faced his father.

"What can I do for you, Dad?"

"I know what you did."

"What's that?" Jake asked, knowingly.

"Seth gave me the check."

"I see."

"He has requested that I divide it in half to repay his account, and the other half to create a new one for you."

"Why did he do that? I've already told him, I don't need the money."

"Your guess is as good as mine, but I thought you should know. Cliff will be stopping by tomorrow to set up a new portfolio for you."

"Thanks for telling me."

"I'm proud of you, Jake."

Jake smiled.

William went to his office, and Jake turned around facing his computer. He thought about what Seth had done. Later that day at lunch, Jake found Seth making a sandwich. He walked up to him at the counter, and extended his hand. Seth saw it, and looked at his brother.

"Thanks, Seth."

Seth understood that Jake knew what he had done with the money. He took his brother's hand in a firm shake.

"What are brothers for?" Seth asked with a grin, placing his left hand on Jake's shoulder.

They smiled at each other in understanding.

"I love you, Seth."

"And I you, little brother."

That's what William witnessed when he entered the kitchen. They turned to have their father putting his arms around both his sons. William had lived to see the day when they became a happy family again.

Epilogue

A year later, Jake and Summer were married on the farm with Seth as his best man, and Summer's sister, Violet, who traveled to be her matron-of-honor. It was a small ceremony with a few close friends of the Abraham's. Not only was it a joyful day for the couple, but a wonderful day for William to witness his youngest son's marriage.

When Jake spoke to his father after six months of dating Summer with the news of his engagement, William was curious if their plans would take him back to the city. However, when Jake told him that he and Summer wished to live on the farm, William knew the perfect place for the newlyweds. He drove Jake to his great-grandfather's house on the rear of the property, the same house he carried his bride over the threshold many years ago.

The house had been closed, but with a crew of men to repair and upgrade, it was renovated into the perfect home, and furnished with new furniture to be ready for occupancy. Jake and Summer were very appreciative, and excited to have a home of their own, and to be close to the business that Jake had an important role in managing.

Summer was loved, and the Abraham men had changed because of her presence. She had a new family now since the death of her parents. Summer graduated with honors, but had no interest in pursuing a career, for all she wanted was a life with Jake. She enjoyed helping in the office working alongside Mrs. Grey, handling her overflow of paperwork and making phone calls to recruit new customers. She couldn't have dreamt of a better life.

Jake was exceedingly grateful for the second chance with his family and with Summer, understanding the value of love and commitment. Seth accepted his fate to be married to the farm and was content with his decision, knowing Jake's children would be the generation to carry the Abraham Organic Farm into the future.

Before celebrating their second anniversary, Summer made a proclamation of the addition to the Abraham family. Jake was ecstatic to hear the news, and once the ultrasound results were in, they were proud to announce their first child would be a boy. Summer wanted to name him in remembrance of her father, so the newest member was named Benjamin Michael Abraham.

William anticipated the day he could take his new grandson, sitting on his lap, to ride the tractor across the Abraham farm just as he had done with his sons. He was very thankful to have lived to see the day broken hearts were mended, and all was well within his family. He was going to see the next generation blossom.

If only Marybeth could see them now, she would be so proud, William thought.

About the Author

Patricia Marlett is dedicated to write inspirational novels for both the adult and young reader genres. With a contemporary platform, she pens plots that reflect real life events reflected through drama, intrigue, suspense, humor, and love. Faith-inspiring messages are subtly weaved in each of her themes lending to heartfelt expressions from laughter to tears and always with hope and encouragement.

Visit Patricia at her website, www.patriciamarlett.com, to learn more, view her books, and for contact information. Also, go to www.Amazon.com to purchase any of her publications.